Candor or Cover-up?

Nikki had gone to her grandfather's house with Tim Cooper on her mind, but when she left, the only person she could think of was Niles Butler. Talk about falling for a guy fast! This had to be a record.

Of course, she hadn't really fallen for him, she told herself. It was just a crush, a case of instant infatuation. If Niles were staying only for a week or so, it wouldn't matter. But he was staying for months. She'd be showing him around town, introducing him to her friends, seeing him at school every day.

It would be great, she thought, except for Tim. Tim was the only one she really cared about . . . wasn't he?

Books in the River Heights ® Series

Available from ARCHWAY Paperbacks

CHEATING HEARTS

CAROLYN KEENE

AN ARCHWAY PAPERBACK
Published by POCKET BOOKS
New York London Toronto Sydney Tokyo Singapore

AN ARCHWAY PAPERBACK *Original*

An Archway Paperback published by
POCKET BOOKS, a division of Simon & Schuster Inc.
1230 Avenue of the Americas, New York, NY 10020

ISBN: 0-671-67765-9

First Archway Paperback printing September 1990

10 9 8 7 6 5 4 3 2 1

 1

Brittany Tate, her dark eyes gleaming curiously, tilted her head and studied Karen Jacobs. "What do you mean, River Heights High might never be the same if this gets out?" Brittany asked. "If what gets out? What happened?"

Karen bit her lip and glanced out the doorway of the newspaper office and down the hall. Not only was Brittany waiting for an answer, but so was Ben Newhouse, the guy Karen was secretly crazy about.

"Well?" Brittany demanded.

"Nothing, really," Karen said. "I heard . . . I mean, I just found out the *Record*'s getting a new advisor." At least that was true, she thought. DeeDee Smith,

1

the school paper's editor in chief, had told her a while ago. "Mr. Green, the social studies teacher, is taking over," Karen went on. "DeeDee said he's got a really strong background in journalism."

"Well, that's very interesting," Brittany said. "But a couple of minutes ago, you looked as if a monster were chasing you down the hall."

"You did look kind of shocked," Ben said to Karen, his brown eyes concerned. "You sure you're okay?"

"Oh, sure." Karen smiled at him. "I guess I was surprised. I mean, we've all gotten used to Mr. McComb, and I kind of forgot he was only filling in until the paper got a permanent advisor."

Karen glanced at Brittany, who was still staring at her. She hoped Brittany believed her. She wasn't about to tell her what had really happened.

Ben was still watching her, too, she noticed. If only she were alone with him, she might tell him the truth. But then again she might not. Not yet, anyway. What she really had to do was get away to think about what she'd just seen.

"Wow!" she said suddenly, glancing at her watch. "I didn't know it was so late. I've got to go or I'll miss the last bus."

With a quick wave, she turned and

dashed down the hall, leaving the other two standing there, totally mystified.

Once she was on her bus, Karen leaned back, took a deep breath, and ran her fingers through her light brown hair. Then she closed her eyes, remembering the incredible scene she'd overheard.

She'd been alone in the *Record* office, working on the layout for the next issue. DeeDee had just told her about the new advisor and then left. Karen had worked for a little while longer, thinking about Ben Newhouse the whole time. Unable to concentrate on anything but him, she'd decided to stop and try to catch her bus home for a change. She'd picked up her books and jacket and was heading for the door when she'd heard voices in the hall.

As the bus rumbled down the street, Karen kept her eyes closed and recalled the conversation she'd heard.

"It's about time," a guy's voice had said. He'd sounded nervous. "I was starting to get worried."

"Hey, we always come through," another guy had said. Karen recognized that voice. It belonged to Jerry Kuperman, one of the stars of the basketball team.

"Now, listen," Jerry went on, "whatever you do, don't ace it. That would look suspicious."

"Oh, sure," the first guy said. "I know that. I don't even need to ace it. All I need is a B, and with this, I know I'll get it."

He'll get a B with what? Karen had wondered. What were they talking about? The door wasn't closed all the way, so she'd peered through the opening. She recognized the other boy. It was Neil Lorrens, a tall, sandy-haired guy who was also on the basketball team. As she watched, Jerry had handed Neil four or five sheets of paper, stapled together.

"This is great," Neil had said, quickly shoving the papers under his jacket. "Now I'll be able to stay on the team."

"Coach is counting on it." Jerry grinned and smoothed back his thick, dark hair.

Neil reached into the back pocket of his jeans. "Twenty?"

Jerry nodded. "And worth every penny, take my word for it." He lowered his voice slightly, but Karen was still able to hear him. "If it wasn't for this, I'd never have passed humanities. I'd be just another tall guy watching from the sidelines."

Neil handed him two bills. Karen could tell he was still very nervous. "And you're sure . . . I mean, this is safe, right?" he'd almost whispered.

"Hey, relax," Jerry had told him. "Nobody's been caught yet." He'd clapped a hand on Neil's shoulder, and the two of them had moved off down the hall.

Now, as the school bus lurched to a halt, Karen opened her eyes. It was her stop. She got off and walked slowly down the sidewalk toward her house.

She still couldn't quite believe what she'd heard, but there was no doubt about what she'd seen. For twenty dollars, Jerry had sold Neil a copy of the humanities exam. And he'd said that nobody had been caught yet. So other kids must be doing this, too.

Karen was shocked, but she was excited, too. This was a story, a big story, and it might be exactly what she needed to get the job of editor in chief for the next year.

Until now, Karen didn't think she'd stand a chance against Brittany Tate. Brittany wrote "Off the Record," the paper's most popular column, plus she did a lot of interviews and lead stories.

Karen was the layout and production editor, and she knew she did a good job, but she didn't have that much writing experience. When DeeDee had told her about the new advisor, Karen hoped she'd be able to do something to impress him.

Now she had a big story handed to her, maybe the biggest, most sensational story to hit River Heights High. She'd been wanting to make her mark on the *Record,* and now she had a way to do it.

"I don't see what you're worried about," Kim Bishop said to Brittany the next morning. The two friends were outside on the quad, waiting for the warning bell. "You're the only one who could possibly take over the paper next year. You don't have any competition."

"Thanks," Brittany said. "But Karen Jacobs wants the job, too. Of course, she doesn't have the nerve to come right out and say so, but I can tell."

"Karen Jacobs?" Kim's blue eyes sparkled with amusement. "She doesn't do anything but get the paper ready for the printer. She doesn't stand a chance."

Brittany had very strong doubts. Karen might be quiet and shy, but she was good at buttering people up. She had DeeDee's support, and she'd probably get the new advisor's, too. Having those two behind her was all she needed to make her editor in chief.

Besides, Brittany hadn't bought Karen's being surprised about the new advisor the day before. Karen was onto a story, Brittany was positive. From the look on Karen's face, Brittany knew the story had to be big.

"Maybe you need a really great story," Kim said. Brushing back her smooth blond hair, she glanced around the crowded quad. When she saw Jerry Kuperman, she said, "How about writing about the basketball team? I hear they're going to be great this year. It could be a pretty big story."

Brittany shook her head. "That kind of story would write itself. I need one I can dig for, so it's my investigative reporting technique that gets noticed." The same story Karen Jacobs is onto, she thought.

"How about Samantha?" Kim asked with a short laugh. "Why don't you do some digging and find out what she's been up to?"

Samantha Daley was their other best friend. Usually she waited out in the quad with Brittany and Kim, and she almost always spent time with one or both of them after school. But she wasn't with them that morning, and neither of them had seen her.

"Haven't you noticed how quiet she's been?" Kim went on.

"Well, she's probably trying to get over her thing for Mr. LeBlanc," Brittany said, mentioning the substitute French teacher Samantha had been in love with. "It's only been a day since she found out he doesn't care about her. She must want to be alone."

The bell rang then, and everyone rushed for the doors. Still discussing what fabulous story Brittany might write, Kim and Brittany didn't even notice the pretty girl with the curly, cinnamon brown hair standing in the stairwell, talking to a boy.

A stairwell was not Samantha Daley's favorite place to hang out. Unfortunately, she couldn't risk being seen with a social zero like Kyle Kirkwood.

"Listen, Samantha," Kyle said, "how come every time I see you, you drag me someplace where nobody can see us? All I wanted to do was ask if you need any more tutoring in French. You couldn't answer me in the hall? You can talk only in a stairwell?"

"Why, Kyle, I don't know what you mean." Samantha had moved to River Heights from the South several years before, and her tone was still soft and lilting. "I just wanted some privacy."

Kyle frowned. "Why?"

With a small sigh, Samantha looked at Kyle. He was smart, and she'd discovered that he had a good sense of humor. His sandy-colored hair and the dimple in his cheek rated him a seven, maybe a seven and a half on the cute scale. But on a social scale, he would be lucky to rate a one. Kyle wasn't quite a nerd, but close. He was tutoring her in French, which was how she'd met him. There was nothing wrong with his being brainy, if only he was a great dancer or dresser or had a great personality, or was terrific at sports. Kyle was none of those things. Samantha was honest with herself—she couldn't possibly risk her reputation by being seen with someone so—what was the right word? *Blah.* That was it. Kyle was socially blah.

"Why did you want privacy?" Kyle asked again.

Samantha shook her head, her curls swaying gently. "Oh, you know what school's like," she told him. "You're seen with somebody and, boom, everybody thinks you're going steady. I didn't think you'd want that."

Kyle laughed. "Look, Samantha, I know everybody thinks I'm a geek," he said. "Nobody would ever believe you'd go steady with me."

Samantha was surprised. She hadn't realized Kyle knew what everyone thought of him. It didn't seem to bother him much, which was also surprising.

"Anyway, even if you don't need any more help in French," he said, "how about going for a doughnut with me after school?"

"Oh, I can't today," Samantha said. Then she shocked herself by saying, "Maybe tomorrow, though."

"Great," Kyle said, his eyes lighting up. "I'll check with you later—or tomorrow."

After Kyle left, Samantha counted to ten before slipping out of the stairwell. There was dust on the arms of her new white sweater. Brushing it off, she tried to figure out why she'd said she might have a doughnut with Kyle. Of course, she'd had a couple of doughnut dates with him before. But that was when he was tutoring her, at Marc LeBlanc's suggestion.

It was only the day before that Samantha had finally realized her crush on Marc LeBlanc was just that—a stupid, schoolgirl crush. She'd cried for a bit, naturally. But she hadn't been totally devastated because she realized she hadn't truly been in love.

Samantha had realized something else, too—she really liked Kyle. If she could just figure out a way to make him into the kind of guy she'd be proud to be seen with, her love life might actually include Kyle Kirkwood!

 **2**

"All right, people." Mr. Viera, the humanities teacher, got up from his desk and walked toward the front row. "That's it. Pass your papers up, please."

A lot of kids groaned and sighed as they turned in their test papers, but Karen noticed that Neil Lorrens wasn't one of them. She'd glanced at him a few times while they were taking the test. He'd stared at the ceiling once or twice, obviously pretending that he was stumped, but she knew it was just an act. How could he be stumped when he'd bought the answers the day before?

Looking around the classroom, Karen wondered if any of the other kids had bought the test answers, too. It was impossible to tell. All she had to go on was what she'd heard Jerry say, that "nobody" had been caught yet. Before she took the story to DeeDee, she wanted to find out how many "nobodies" were involved.

She'd thought of something else, too. Neil told Jerry that passing this test would keep him on the basketball team, and Jerry said, "Coach is counting on it."

Could the coach, Mike Shay, possibly know about this whole cheating thing? Could he even be helping so he wouldn't lose any players because of grades? Mr. Shay was extremely popular at school. He was young and good-looking and out to win.

Just then, Karen felt a hand on her shoulder. She turned and stared up into the brown eyes of Ben Newhouse. For a moment she forgot everything except how much she cared about him.

"Are you in shock from the test?" he asked with a grin. "The bell rang, and you're still sitting here."

Feeling herself blush, Karen laughed a little. "I can't believe I didn't hear it," she said, gathering her notebooks and getting up. "I guess I was thinking too hard."

"I'm surprised you've got any brainpower left," Ben joked as they walked out of the classroom together. "That test just about wiped me out."

Karen couldn't think of anything to say, mainly because Ben still had his hand on her shoulder. Feeling it there pushed everything else out of her mind.

"Listen," he said, "how about if we eat lunch together today?"

"I'd like that," Karen told him. Would she ever!

"Great. Whoever gets there first takes a taste test to make sure the food's not poisoned." Ben gave her shoulder a little squeeze and smiled down at her before taking off.

Karen stood still for a moment, watching him make his way down the hall and smiling to herself. Not only had Ben asked her to eat lunch with him, but now she didn't have to spend the rest of the morning thinking of things to talk about. She'd wanted to tell him about the cheating story the day before, but with Brittany standing there, she couldn't. Ben understood how much Karen wanted to be editor in chief the next year, and maybe he'd have some ideas about the best way to investigate and write the story.

But the most important thing was just being with him. Karen was glad she'd worn her green turtleneck because it brought out the green in her hazel eyes. Maybe he'd notice that instead of her hair, which was frizzier than usual.

Still smiling, Karen headed for her next class, counting the minutes till lunch.

Nikki Masters blew a lock of blond hair out of her eyes, brought the camera up, focused, and took four fast shots. Coach Shay blew his whistle, and the basketball players suddenly pivoted and began racing to the other end of the court, their shoes squeaking loudly on the polished wooden floor of the gym. The coach, his curly dark hair covered by a faded baseball cap, ran with them, calling out instructions and encouragement. Because the games were to begin soon, the team was practicing every chance it could get. They'd all given up their lunch periods just to get in some extra work.

Nikki jumped out of the players' way, then ran over to the first row of bleachers, where her best friends, Robin Fisher and Lacey Dupree, were sitting.

"I never realized taking pictures could be hazardous to your health," Robin said, her brown eyes crinkling as she grinned.

"Robin's right," Lacey agreed. "You almost got trampled out there, Nikki."

"I know." Nikki reached into her camera bag. "Since it was my idea to take these pictures, I can't chicken out now. Besides," she added, "it keeps me busy. I'd rather be doing this than sitting in the cafeteria right now."

Robin and Lacey exchanged glances. They both knew why Nikki was avoiding the cafeteria—Tim Cooper would be there. Nikki and Tim had just broken up. It had been a messy breakup. Because of some sly hints from Brittany Tate, Nikki thought Tim was interested in another girl, and then Tim accused Nikki of not trusting him.

Frowning, Robin fluffed up her short dark hair and leaned closer to Nikki. "Listen," she said. "It's not like you and Tim aren't speaking. I mean, you told me that you actually had a conversation the other day. So how come you're still trying to keep out of his way?"

"It's not that." Nikki sighed as she ripped open a new roll of film. "It's just that the cafeteria's so public, you know? I feel like everybody's watching us to see how we act with each other."

"How *do* you act with each other?" Lacey asked.

"Sort of like we're not sure whether to shake hands or come out swinging," Nikki said. "No, it's not that bad, really. But I'd rather not have the entire cafeteria as an audience."

Having finished loading her camera, Nikki jumped off the bench and ran back onto the floor.

"Okay, guys!" Coach Shay shouted. "You're looking sloppy! Get it together!"

"He's really putting the pressure on," Lacey commented.

"Mmm. Do you think Nikki and Tim will get back together?" Robin asked Lacey, taking a big bite of apple. Both of them had brought fruit and crackers since they'd decided to spend their lunch period with Nikki. "I get the feeling Nikki wants to," she added.

Lacey tossed back the long hair that framed her face in a halo of red waves. "I'm not sure Nikki really knows what she wants," she said. "If she wanted to get back with Tim, I think she'd be in the cafeteria instead of here."

"Maybe." Robin chewed another bite of apple and stretched out her long, slender legs. "So where's Rick?" she asked. "He has lunch now."

"He's in the library, working on a paper for English," Lacey said, a small frown appearing between her light blue eyes as she thought of her boyfriend, Rick Stratton.

"What's wrong?" Robin asked, noticing the frown.

"I'm not sure. Maybe nothing," Lacey said with a shrug. "It's just that lately Rick always seems to find an excuse to be by himself."

"Well, he can't do research and talk to you at the same time," Robin pointed out. "And didn't you say he's going to apply to some really top-notch colleges next year? He's probably been studying like crazy."

"Probably," Lacey said doubtfully. "But you know how he likes to hike and how he's always trying to talk me into going along?"

Robin nodded and grinned. Lacey wasn't lazy, but hiking wasn't her favorite activity. In fact, no outdoor activity was high on her list of fun things to do.

"Well, he's stopped asking," Lacey said. "And he's gotten really quiet."

"Lacey, Rick's always been quiet," Robin reminded her. "And you ought to be glad he's not bugging you to put on twenty-pound hiking boots and scramble around on some rocky slope!"

"I guess you're right." Lacey smiled. "And we *are* going to the basketball game Friday night. Maybe I've just been imagining things."

"You're going to the game? So are Cal

and I," Robin said, mentioning Calvin Roth, her boyfriend. "He's really excited about the team this season."

"The whole school's excited," Lacey remarked. "I guess it's catching."

"Okay, okay!" the coach shouted. "That's a little better! Don't forget to talk to one another out there!"

"Just think," Robin said as Coach Shay's whistle blew. "Maybe they'll be good enough to get in the state championship. If that doesn't put River Heights High on the map, nothing will!"

The cafeteria was crowded and noisy, as usual, but Karen hardly noticed. With Ben Newhouse sitting across from her, everything else faded away.

Ben had gotten to the cafeteria first, and when Karen came off the food line with her tray, he'd stood up and waved so she could see him. Threading her way through the tables, Karen saw several people look back and forth between her and Ben. She was so happy, she had to stop herself from grinning like an idiot.

Now, halfway through his tuna sandwich, Ben stopped eating and smiled at her. "Okay," he said. "I've been talking since you sat down. Now it's your turn."

"Well, you have kind of monopolized the

conversation," Karen said jokingly. "But I don't mind, really." That was true. Ben was involved in a lot of school activities, and he was enthusiastic about them all. He was really big on school spirit, but he was so sincere about it that nobody thought he was corny.

"I get carried away, I guess. Anyway, you've got something on your mind, I can tell by your eyes." He leaned across the table, peering into her face. "They're green!" he said, sounding surprised. "I never noticed before."

"They're hazel, actually," Karen told him, feeling as if she might float up from her chair. "It's my sweater that makes them seem greener."

"Well, whatever," Ben said. "I can still tell there's something on your mind."

"You're right," Karen agreed. She pushed aside the rest of her salad and folded her arms on the table. "Remember yesterday, when I ran into you and Brittany outside the *Record* office?"

Ben nodded. "Yeah, you looked really freaked."

"I was," Karen told him. "I didn't want to say anything then, but I stumbled across something really big," she said. "It's a story, an incredible story."

She had Ben's full attention now. He

folded his arms on the table, too, and leaned closer. "Don't keep me in suspense," he said. "Tell me."

Starting at the very beginning, from when she'd heard Jerry and Neil talking in the hall the afternoon before, Karen told him the story.

"I have to get a lot more information, of course," she finished. "Like how many kids are involved, and how they get the tests, and whether Coach Shay knows about it. Is it just guys on the team, or is it anybody who's willing to pay twenty dollars?"

Karen took a deep breath and drank some juice. "A cheating ring," she said. "You hear about them all the time, but I guess I never thought it would happen here at River Heights High. It's the biggest story I've heard since I've been here."

Karen smiled across the table at Ben. "Well, that's it," she said. "That's what's been on my mind. What do you think?"

Ben stared at her for a minute, a serious expression on his face. Finally, he said, "Who else have you told about this?"

"Nobody, not even DeeDee yet," Karen said. "You're the first."

To her surprise, Ben let out a big sigh of relief. "Well, that's good news," he said.

"What do you mean?"

Ben leaned even closer to her. "Karen, you can't write that story."

If her chin hadn't been in her hands, Karen's mouth would have fallen open in surprise. "But . . . why not?"

"Don't you see? Something like that'll rip the school apart," Ben said.

"But, Ben, this is a cheating ring," Karen said. "Kids are getting the answers to tests and selling them to other kids! It's terrible. Why shouldn't it be exposed?"

"I know it's terrible," Ben agreed. "But ruining people's lives is terrible, too, and that's what'll happen if you write it. There has to be a better way to deal with it."

Before Karen could think of anything to say, Ben reached out and took her hand. "Promise me something, Karen," he said. "Promise you won't write this story until I have a chance to think. I'm sure I can come up with some way for you to . . . hint about what's going on without exposing everybody." He squeezed her hand tightly. "Will you do that for me, Karen?"

Suddenly Karen couldn't feel anything but the warmth of his hand. He'd never held her hand before. Sure, he was asking for a favor, but Ben Newhouse wouldn't hold anybody's hand unless he cared, would he?

What did a day or two matter, anyway?

The cheating had probably been going on for a long time; it wasn't going to stop now. Karen wasn't sure there was any other way to deal with the story, but she was willing to give Ben a chance to try.

"Okay, Ben," she said quietly. "I'll wait."

At that moment the bell rang. Scraping their chairs back, Karen and Ben got up and headed for the door. Neither of them noticed Brittany Tate sitting off to the side of them.

Brittany had been listening to Samantha going on about some cousin of hers down South. The cousin apparently had a crush on a real loser, and Samantha was trying to come up with ways for the cousin to turn him into a winner.

The whole conversation was pretty boring. Brittany wasn't particularly interested in losers, and she'd tuned Samantha out about halfway through her story. That's when she heard Karen Jacobs say something to Ben Newhouse about a cheating ring.

Now, *that* was interesting. Brittany had leaned back in her chair as far as she could without falling over.

Ben had said something about ruining people's lives and not writing the story. Brittany couldn't catch much, but the last thing she heard was Karen saying she'd wait.

Good, Brittany thought, her mouth curving in a smile. That would give her time to find out exactly what was going on. Once she did, the story would be hers.

3 ～～

After school on Wednesday, Nikki dropped five rolls of film off at the *Record* office before heading out to the student parking lot. As she walked toward her metallic blue Camaro, she caught herself peering around, and she realized she was looking for Tim Cooper.

Stop it, she told herself. You don't even know what to say to him these days. If you ran into him, you'd stammer for a few seconds and then make some dumb comment about the weather.

With a sigh, Nikki climbed into her car and headed home. Would she and Tim ever get back together? They were talking again, but it wasn't the same as before. She hoped it would be, someday, but she had no idea how Tim felt. That was the worst —not knowing how he felt. Before the breakup, she always seemed to know what he was thinking.

She had to stop thinking about it and him. Thank goodness she had a pile of homework, and she was going over to Lacey's later to study. That ought to keep her mind off Tim Cooper.

Nikki turned into the driveway of her house and parked by the front door. Letting herself into the handsome Tudor house, she ran up the stairs to her bedroom. It was a light, airy room, with a polished wood floor, a bright quilt on the bed, and several of Nikki's best photographs on the walls.

There was also a big corkboard on the wall above the desk, where Nikki kept ticket stubs, to-do lists, snapshots, programs, and a calendar. She dropped her books on the desk and was just about to flop on the bed when the calendar caught her eye.

"Oh, no, not tonight!" she cried.

There it was, written in black Magic Marker: Grandfather's—7:30 dinner. There was also the word *formal,* underlined twice.

Nikki immediately reached for the bedside phone and punched the number of the record store where Lacey worked after school.

"Platters," Lacey answered.

"Hi, Lacey, it's Nikki. I can't come over to study with you tonight."

"Why? What's wrong?" Lacey asked.

"Nothing," Nikki said. "Except my grandfather's giving this dinner for some business associate from England and I promised I'd go. I'm sorry, Lacey. I completely forgot about it."

"Oh, that's okay," Lacey said. "But you don't usually go to business-type dinners."

"I know," Nikki said, leaning back against the pillows. "But this man—I can't remember his name—has his family with him, and my grandfather asked if my parents and I would come so they'd have somebody to talk to. I'm really not in the mood to make conversation, but I have to be there."

"You said they're from England, though, so maybe it'll be kind of interesting," Lacey said. "Listen, this place is getting busy," she added. "I have to go. Try to have fun tonight and I'll see you tomorrow, okay?"

"Okay. 'Bye, Lacey." After Nikki hung up, she scooted off the bed and walked over to her closet. Formal didn't mean a floor-length gown, of course, but she couldn't show up in a sweater and jeans and high-tops.

She pulled out a dress still swathed in dry-cleaner's plastic that would be just right—midnight blue velvet, with long sleeves and buttons down the back.

Now she had to hurry and shower, then do as much homework as possible before it was time to go. As Nikki undressed and slipped into her white terry cloth robe, she decided the dinner party might not be so bad, after all. Being with her grandfather was always fun, the food would be great, and as Lacey had said, the people from England might be interesting. The best part was that it would take her mind off Tim Cooper.

Karen rummaged in the refrigerator and brought out two cans of soda and a tub of cheese spread. She got crackers and a knife and set it all on the kitchen table in front of her best friend, Teresa D'Amato.

Teresa peered at the food over the top of her calculus book. "Great," she said, her dark eyes lighting up. "I might get through this after all." She spread some cheese on a cracker and wolfed it down. "There are times I wish I'd never heard of calculus, and this is one of them. This class is going to kill me."

Karen popped the tab on her soda and sat down. "I wish I could help, but I'm just not cut out for higher math."

"I'm beginning to think I'm not, either." Teresa leaned back and ran her fingers through her dark brown hair. "If I don't start doing better, I might have to get outside help."

Karen frowned. "What do you mean?"

"I mean like a tutor." Teresa laughed.

"Oh, right."

"What's with you tonight, anyway?" Teresa asked, reaching for another cracker. "I thought you'd be flying. I mean, you had lunch with Ben! But you're not even acting excited about it."

"Oh, I'm excited," Karen said slowly. "It's just that . . ." She stopped and thought for a minute. Ben had asked her not to tell anyone about the cheating story. But was he right? Should she not write the story at all? She just didn't know.

"Listen, Terry," Karen went on, "I need some advice. About Ben."

"Good." Teresa slapped her book closed and propped her elbows on the table.

"This'll be much more interesting than calculus!"

"I can't tell you all the details," Karen said. "But I discovered something that's going on, and I want to do a story on it. It's a big story, really important. Plus it would help my chances for being appointed editor in chief next year." Seeing the curiosity on Teresa's face, she held up her hand. "Please, don't ask me what it is. I just can't tell you. Not yet, anyway."

"Well, okay," Teresa agreed. "But what's this got to do with Ben?"

"I told him about it, and he doesn't think I should write about it," Karen said with a sigh. "He thinks it's the wrong way to go, and he was very serious about it."

"But you're not sure?" Teresa asked.

Karen shook her head.

"And you think Ben will get mad if you go ahead and write it?"

"You guessed it," Karen said with a little grin. "I guess I'm just not sure the story's worth losing my chances with Ben. Do you think I'm crazy?"

"Are you kidding?" Teresa said. "Karen, you're a junior already. This is the first time you've really had a boyfriend. Well, an 'almost' boyfriend. And it's Ben Newhouse! I think you'd be crazy to risk it."

"What about the story?"

"Can't you give it to somebody else to write?"

"I'd hate to do that," Karen said. "Anyway, Ben would know. He doesn't want it written by anybody."

"This is really frustrating," Teresa complained. "I wish you could tell me what this mysterious story is." She paused. "It must be something bad," she went on, reaching for another cracker. "Otherwise, Ben wouldn't want you to keep quiet about it. And if it's bad, somebody else will probably find out about it sooner or later, right?"

"Maybe," Karen said with a shrug.

"Sure they will," Teresa said. "You know all those crooks on Wall Street— they did all that illegal stuff for years, but eventually, somebody found out and blew the whistle. It'll happen with your story, too." She took a sip of soda and grinned. "So if you just wait it out, the story will get written. Best of all, you'll still have Ben Newhouse!"

"You're probably right," Karen said slowly. "I just wish I could be sure."

Carefully, Samantha leaned around the pillar in the Westmoor University library and checked out the rest of the tables.

Good. Nobody she recognized was there. Relieved, she took off the itchy wool cap and shook her hair free. Then she shrugged out of the huge, ugly dark coat she'd found way at the back of the hall closet. She was pretty sure it was a coat her father had been meaning to get rid of. It smelled of mothballs, and it hung on her like a tent, but it made a great cover-up. Glad to be out of it, she walked across the room to where Kyle was sitting.

"Hi," she said with a brilliant smile.

"I saw you come in," Kyle said, pulling out a chair for her. He frowned at the coat and gave her a curious glance. "You looked like somebody in disguise."

"Don't be silly," Samantha told him. "I just ran out of the house in such a hurry that I didn't notice what coat I grabbed." She tossed the horrible coat on a chair and sat down next to it. "Have you been waiting long?"

"A few minutes," Kyle said, "but that's okay. This is a pretty good library. I already found all the books I'll need to do my psychology paper."

"Great." Now Samantha didn't feel so guilty. When she'd agreed to meet him for a study date, she suggested Westmoor because she knew most kids from school used the River Heights Library.

"Too bad I won't be able to check any of them out," Kyle added, going back to work.

"Oh." Feeling guilty, Samantha pulled out her English book and pretended to study, but she couldn't concentrate. Something had to be done about this situation with Kyle, and it was up to her to figure out what. Brittany hadn't been any help at all. She'd barely listened today at lunch when Samantha was telling her about her "cousin."

Actually, though, it was probably just as well. If Brittany *had* been paying attention, she might have guessed that the "cousin" didn't exist. Brittany was very good at sniffing out the truth.

Lost in thought, Samantha jumped when a voice said, "Psst!" She raised her head to find Kyle smiling at her.

"That must be a pretty interesting assignment," he said. "I've been trying to get your attention for five minutes."

Closing her book, Samantha leaned across the table. "You've got my attention now," she said softly. "What is it?"

"I guess you know about the basketball game Friday night," he said.

"Sure. The whole school's psyched for it," Samantha said. "Our first game this

year. I didn't think you were a fan,
though."

"I know, I know," Kyle said, rolling his
eyes. "I'm a geek, right? Geeks know zip
about sports."

"I didn't mean that!" Samantha protested. But that was exactly what she'd been
thinking, and she felt guilty all over again.

"Anyway," Kyle went on, "I happen to
be a geek who goes for basketball. So
would you like to go to the game with
me?"

Oh, no. She couldn't, she just couldn't.
Everybody she knew would be there.
There was no way she could disguise her-
self well enough.

"Oh, Kyle, I'm sorry," Samantha said,
her brown eyes filled with disappointment.
"I wish I could, but I promised a friend I'd
go with her." That wasn't quite true, but
she and Brittany *had* discussed it. And
Friday night was Jeremy Pratt's big party.
She would have loved to take Kyle, but that
was impossible. "I really can't back out on
her," she said.

"That's okay," Kyle said. But he ap-
peared to be disappointed and slightly suspicious, too.

He's not going to put up with this much
longer, Samantha told herself. He's going

to realize that you're embarrassed by him, and then he's going to walk right out of your life.

Almost without thinking, Samantha said, "I'm going to the mall on Saturday, and I'd really love some company. If you're not too busy, that is."

Kyle's expression changed immediately. "Well, sure," he said happily. "That'd be great. What time should I pick you up?"

"Why don't we just meet there?" Samantha suggested quickly. She still wasn't ready to be seen in Kyle's awful van. "I have a couple of errands to run first. Is eleven o'clock okay?"

"Sure. At the fountain?"

"Wonderful." Samantha gulped. The fountain was where everybody gathered; not getting spotted there was going to be tricky. Not getting spotted *anywhere* was going to be tricky, since hundreds of kids cruised the mall on Saturday. Why on earth had she ever suggested it?

Already trying to decide how to disguise herself without being too obvious, Samantha watched Kyle as he got up to put a book back on a shelf.

Look at the guy, she thought in despair. Brown corduroy pants and a long-sleeved polo shirt with a brown stripe in it. To go with the pants, of course. Matching stuff like that was just not cool.

And his hair! Kyle had such great hair, thick and sandy blond, but there was absolutely no style to the cut. It was as if he just closed his eyes and chopped away with a pair of shears. No, Kyle's hair was hopeless.

There was no question about it. Kyle was a nice guy—but he was a fashion catastrophe!

4

"How's my girl?" Nikki's grandfather pulled her to him and gave her a big hug. Then he held her away and smiled, his blue eyes twinkling. "How's that car I gave you holding up?"

"We're both doing fine, Grandfather," Nikki said with a laugh, kissing him on the cheek. "How are you?"

"Couldn't be better." He kissed Nikki's mother and shook hands with his son, Nikki's father. "My family's here, and business is booming."

Nikki's father smiled. "I gather Charles Butler is doing great things with Masters Electronics in Great Britain."

Butler, Nikki remembered, as her grandfather's maid took their coats. That was the name of the people they were meeting tonight.

"He sure is," her grandfather said. "And while Charles is here, the three of us can work up some plans for expansion."

"Not over dinner, I hope," Nikki's mother said. "Don't you get your fill of business at the office?"

Nikki's grandfather laughed, too. "I never get my fill of it, Victoria."

That was true, Nikki thought. Her grandfather clearly enjoyed his work. That was probably the main reason Masters Electronics was a multimillion-dollar success.

"Well, let's go into the library, shall we?" the elder Mr. Masters said, gesturing toward two big wooden doors at the end of the large foyer. "I'll introduce you to the Butlers, and we can all chat a little before dinner."

As Nikki and her family walked into the library, with its beautiful Oriental rug and ceiling-high bookshelves, three people turned to them.

Mrs. Butler, a small, light-haired woman with big brown eyes, smiled and rose from the leather couch.

Charles Butler, a tall man with graying

hair and a friendly face, got up from one of the big club chairs and walked over to them, holding out his hand.

Their son, Niles, was standing by the fireplace. As he moved toward Nikki, she felt her mouth go dry and her heart start to pound. As the visitor from England took her hand and smiled at her with chestnut-colored eyes, all thoughts of Tim Cooper flew from Nikki's mind. Niles Butler was the best-looking guy Nikki had ever seen —ever.

After a few minutes of small talk dinner was announced, and they all went into the dining room. Nikki sat silently through the seafood bisque. She hoped she didn't seem rude, but just listening to Niles Butler's beautiful accent was all she wanted to do.

Finally, Niles smiled at her from across the gleaming mahogany dining table. "I understand that you're interested in photography, Nikki," he said.

Nikki nodded. "I take a lot of pictures." What a clever answer, she thought, reaching for her water goblet. Think of something better to say or you'll put him to sleep. She gulped some water and cleared her throat. "I do a lot of work for my school paper, but what I really like is just

walking around with my camera and finding interesting shots.''

"That's exactly what I like to do," Niles
told her. "I bought my first camera when I
was six, with my birthday money. I took
about a hundred rolls of film where I cut
people's heads off," he added with a smile.

Nikki smiled, too, but once again she
couldn't think of anything to say. It was
ridiculous—she knew enough about photography to converse with a professional.
Instead, she just sat there, mute, feeling
her face get redder and redder.

If Niles noticed that she was tongue-
tied, he didn't let on. Turning to Nikki's
mother, he asked about her painting and
soon the two of them were having a lively
discussion about modern art.

Nikki ate her swordfish steak automati-
cally. It was one of her favorites, but that
night it might as well have been grilled
cardboard. She hardly tasted a bite.

She knew she was acting like a twelve-
year-old with a crush, but she couldn't
help it. First, Niles Butler had nearly
blown her away with his looks—thick,
chestnut brown hair, dark-lashed eyes to
match, and the kind of intimate smile that
made her feel as if she were the only one in
the room.

Then Niles had turned out to be not only good-looking, but bright and funny and charming. His manners made those of most of the guys at school seem totally cloddish, and sexy was the only word for his British accent.

Reaching for her water goblet again, Nikki glanced up and caught her grandfather staring at her. His eyes were crinkled in a smile, and she had a feeling he knew exactly how she felt. She just hoped her feelings weren't so obvious to everyone else. Thank goodness for the candlelight —maybe nobody could see her blushing.

"Nikki," her grandfather said in a jovial tone, "did I mention that the Butlers are going to be in River Heights for a while? Several months, in fact?"

"Uh, no, Grandfather, you didn't tell me that." Nikki gulped.

"They've rented a house a few blocks from here. Niles is all set to become a junior at River Heights High," Mr. Masters explained.

"Next week, I hope," Niles said, picking up the conversation. "And I must admit, I'm slightly nervous about the whole thing."

"That's understandable," Nikki's grandfather said. "After all, you'll be starting in an entirely different school system, doing new things, meeting new people." He leaned back in his chair and grinned at Nikki again. "But I'm sure my granddaughter will be happy to show you around and introduce you to her friends. Won't you, Nikki?"

"Yes, of course," Nikki said. Helping Niles Butler out would hardly be a chore, she thought.

"In fact," her grandfather went on, "you might want to start sooner than next week, Nikki. If you're not too busy, you could take Niles around River Heights over the weekend. Take him to a few of the places you kids like to go to. Isn't there a basketball game Friday night?"

"I'd like that very much," Niles said. "I confess I'm quite ignorant about the game. Not as ignorant as I am about baseball, but close." He stopped, looking embarrassed. "But I'm sure you must have already made plans, Nikki, so please don't feel obligated."

"Oh, no, it's okay!" Hearing how enthusiastic she sounded, Nikki blushed again. "I mean, I *do* have plans to go to the game, but it's with a group of good friends. They're all nice, and it'll work out fine because you'll have a chance to get to know them while I'm busy taking pictures."

"It's a date, then," her grandfather said.

"Yes," Niles agreed, smiling at Nikki. "It's a date."

Samantha was lying on her bed, staring at the ceiling. It just wasn't fair. Here she was stuck with a problem, and she couldn't even share it with her best friends.

Brittany and Kim could give great advice, but this was one situation they'd never understand. Samantha's friends prided themselves on their popularity. They would laugh in Samantha's face if she told them she cared about a dweeb like Kyle Kirkwood.

The worst part was that Kyle wasn't bad-looking. With a few changes, he could be a total knockout. But how did you tell a guy that he was breaking every fashion rule in the book?

Frustrated, Samantha rolled over and pulled a fashion magazine from her nightstand. The cover featured a model wearing a swimsuit on a Caribbean beach. Samantha sighed, wishing she were anywhere but River Heights.

Leafing through the magazine, she came to an article on women who had undergone fashion make-overs.

The minute her eyes lit on the title, it

was as if a light bulb had flashed on in her brain.

"The Great American Make-over." She read the headline, and her heart began to race. "A New You from Head to Toe."

"That's it!" Samantha sat up in bed and clapped her hands together.

It was perfect! If Kyle Kirkwood needed a fashion image, she'd give him one!

The article showed how someone's overall look could change with a new wardrobe and hairstyle.

There was one woman with waist-length hair who had had it cut quite short. Another woman with gray hair ended up a brunette. And a third woman, once dressed in a drab navy suit, was now decked out in a black miniskirt with a hot pink top.

A fashion make-over would do wonders for Kyle, and what better place to change someone's look than at the mall? Maybe her Saturday date with Kyle was actually a blessing in disguise!

She'd have to be subtle about it, of course. She couldn't just come out and tell him he needed a complete make-over. But she could steer him into a few clothes stores, maybe even pick out a few outfits that would look good on him. . . .

Jumping up from her bed, Samantha

then ran over to her desk for a notepad. It always helped to make a list of things to be done—that way she wouldn't miss anything.

Item #1: jeans and sweater
Item #2: shoes
Item #3: haircut
Item #4: jacket

She hated the dopey jacket Kyle always wore. It was an ugly green color—the kind of jacket someone's mother would choose.

Leaning back, Samantha reviewed her list. It seemed so easy, she wanted to laugh.

She wished she could call Brittany or Kim and share the good news, but that was impossible. Still, if things went according to her plan, they'd know soon enough that she was interested in Kyle Kirkwood. In the new Kyle Kirkwood, of course.

Saturday was the day. If all went well, it would take just one trip to the mall to create a new Kyle Kirkwood—from head to toe!

In her room later that night, Nikki changed into her soft terry cloth robe, propped herself up in bed, and opened her

copy of *Macbeth*. For the first time since
they'd started reading the play in English
class, it made no sense to her.

Niles Butler was the reason she couldn't
concentrate, of course. She'd gone to her
grandfather's house with Tim Cooper on
her mind, but when she'd left, the only
person she could think of was Niles Butler. Talk about falling for a guy fast! This
had to be a record.

Of course, she hadn't really fallen for
him, she told herself. It was just a crush, a
case of instant infatuation. If Niles were
staying only for a week or so, it wouldn't
matter. But he was staying for months.
She'd be showing him around town, introducing him to her friends, seeing him at
school every day.

It would be great, she thought, except for
Tim. Tim was the one she cared about,
wasn't he?

Nikki reached for her bedside phone,
but she put it down when she noticed the
time. Eleven-thirty. Too late to call Robin
or Lacey.

Okay, she didn't have to figure it out this
very minute. She could talk to them in the
morning. Dropping *Macbeth* onto the floor,
she shrugged out of her robe, turned off the
bedside light, and settled down to sleep.

Five minutes later she sat up, put her robe back on, and went downstairs to the kitchen.

Munching cookies and sipping milk, Nikki wondered if she should tell Niles about Tim. Not every detail, of course. She'd just casually tell him that she was dating someone else, or rather, that she had been until a couple weeks ago, and that she wasn't completely free. Just in case Niles thought she was.

No, that was ridiculous. Just because Niles called going to the basketball game "a date" didn't mean he really thought of it as *a date*. She'd look like a complete fool if she made a big deal about Tim and then found out Niles wasn't even interested in her.

But as she ate another cookie, Nikki found herself hoping that he was.

"So what's the problem?" Robin asked, as Nikki drove her and Lacey to school Thursday morning. "You're just showing this Niles guy around, aren't you? You're being nice. It's not like you're dating him."

"I know." Nikki sighed. "It's just that—"

"It's just that Tim might think she *is* dating him," Lacey put in. "And things are shaky enough between her and Tim right now."

"Exactly," Nikki agreed.

Robin shook her head. "I still don't see the problem."

Lacey leaned forward from the back seat. "The problem is, Nikki's interested in Niles," she explained to Robin. "At least, she might be, if she didn't have Tim to think about. But she does have Tim to think about, and she doesn't want to give either one of them the wrong idea."

"Exactly," Nikki said again.

"And," Lacey went on, "Nikki's got to know how she feels before she decides what to do."

"Oh. Right." Robin turned to Nikki. "How *do* you feel?"

"I don't know!" Nikki wailed. "That's the problem. I never expected to fall for anybody—especially for anybody at a dinner at my grandfather's. I'm not even sure I really did fall. Plus, I still care about Tim. At least, I'm pretty sure I do," she added.

Robin clapped a hand over her dark hair and let out a whistle.

"You see?" Lacey said. "It's not as simple as it sounds."

By this time Nikki was pulling into the parking lot. "Quick, guys!" she said. "Help me figure out what to do, okay? I can't go through the whole day worrying about this."

"Okay," Robin said. "Here goes— you're interested in Niles, right?"

Nikki bit her lip. "I think so."

"Okay. You tell Niles about Tim. But you also ask Tim how he feels about your seeing somebody else. You don't have to go into every last detail," she added. "But it's only fair to ask him."

"Robin's right," Lacey said as Nikki switched off the ignition. "Be honest with everybody, right at the very beginning. That way there won't be any confusion or hurt feelings later on, no matter what happens."

"Okay," Nikki agreed. "I guess I knew that was what I'd have to do all along. Thanks for spelling it out for me."

"No problem," Robin said with a grin.

Nikki felt a little better, but Lacey's words kept running through her mind— "no matter what happens."

Nikki couldn't help wondering what *was* going to happen. Not so much with Tim. But what was going to happen with her and Niles Butler?

 **5**

Before lunch on Thursday, Karen went into the bathroom to brush her hair. She took the brush out of her bag and stared at herself in the mirror. Her hair didn't look too bad, actually. It wasn't as frizzy as usual since she'd had it trimmed a couple of weeks before. But she looked a little tired. And no wonder. Trying to figure out what to do with the cheating story had made her lose sleep.

While she was staring at herself, Ellen Ming, the junior class treasurer, came in.

"Hi, Karen," Ellen said, taking out a comb and running it through her silky dark hair. "How's Ben?"

"Ben?"

"You know—Ben Newhouse, junior

49

class president? Really nice, good-looking?" Ellen laughed. "Just a few weeks ago, in this very bathroom, you told me how much you liked him. I just wondered how things were going, that's all."

"Sorry," Karen said with a smile. "I'm just not with it today."

That was an understatement, she thought. She'd hardly slept at all. Before she went to bed, she was sure that Teresa was right—the story wasn't worth risking her chances with Ben.

But after she'd turned out the lights and thought for a while, she wasn't sure anymore. The story was really important, and not just for her, either. The more she thought about kids buying answers to tests, the madder she got. Most kids worked hard for their grades, and a few kids shouldn't be allowed to buy their way through school. It just wasn't fair.

Why didn't Ben see it that way?

Karen glanced in the mirror and saw Ellen staring at her curiously. The two of them weren't close friends, but Ellen was honest and up-front about things. Karen needed more advice, and she decided to trust Ellen.

"Could I talk to you about something?" she asked. "It's kind of important, and I can't tell you everything, but I'd really like your opinion."

"Sure, Karen. What is it?"

Just then a group of girls came in, so Karen said, "I'll tell you in the hall, okay?"

The hall was crowded, too, but everybody was talking about classes or the game Friday, so Karen didn't worry about being overheard.

"Now," Ellen said when they found a fairly quiet spot next to some lockers. "Tell me."

As she had with Teresa, Karen kept the actual story to herself. She admitted that it was a big story, and that it could hurt some people. "But they're doing something wrong," she said. "So maybe they deserve to be exposed."

"Sure they do," Ellen said quickly. "People shouldn't be allowed to get away with—whatever they're getting away with."

"But maybe there's a better way to stop them than with a newspaper story," Karen said. "Ben thinks I'd be wrong to write it."

"You mean Ben really wants you to censor yourself?" Ellen asked. "I can't believe it. This is freedom of the press you're talking about, Karen. If something bad's going on, you owe it to the school to let everyone know. I'm really surprised Ben doesn't agree with you. You want me to talk to him?"

"Oh, no, please don't do that," Karen said quickly. "I'll talk to him myself. I just wanted somebody else's opinion. Thanks, Ellen."

"Sure," Ellen said. "See you later."

Now she had three opinions, Karen thought as she headed for the cafeteria. All of them were different. If only she had a strong opinion of her own, she might be able to decide what to do.

For the tenth time Nikki glanced through the doorway of the cafeteria. Tim was still there, at a table with Brian Cotter and Doug Lynch. They were finished eating, but they kept on sitting and talking.

Nikki nervously shifted her books from one arm to the other. She wished they'd hurry up and finish their conversation. She had to talk to Tim before the day was over and he saw her at the basketball game Friday night with Niles Butler.

Robin and Lacey had been right, of course. Things were shaky enough between her and Tim for her suddenly to be seen with somebody else. If Niles was interested in her—not that he definitely was—then she had to tell him about Tim. Nikki sighed. She knew what she had to do, but it wasn't going to be easy.

She was choosing the right words to use when she suddenly noticed that Tim was standing right in front of her.

"I thought that was you," he said, a curious look in his gray eyes. "You've been standing out here for ten minutes. Are you waiting for someone?"

"Well, yes. You." Nikki laughed nervously. "I need to talk to you."

"Okay, sure." He checked his watch. "I left a book in my locker. Why don't you walk there with me and we can talk on the way?"

It felt almost like old times, walking down the hall with Tim Cooper at her side. Nikki half expected him to put his hand on her shoulder, the way he used to. But it wasn't old times, of course, so Tim kept his hands in his pockets.

"So," he said after a moment, "you wanted to talk?"

"Yes." Nikki cleared her throat and stole a quick glance up at him. He was staring straight ahead and she had no idea what he was thinking.

"Tim, I was wondering something." Nikki stopped and cleared her throat again. This wasn't going to be easy. "I wanted to know . . . I mean, well, how things stand between us. Or how you think they stand."

Now Tim glanced at her quickly before turning away. "I don't know, Nikki," he said. "How do *you* think things stand between us?"

"This is embarrassing," Nikki said, taking a deep breath. "I'm not sure about us," she blurted out. "I don't know what's going to happen, or even what I want to happen."

Tim nodded. "That's about the way I feel, I guess." They were at his locker now, and he was rummaging on the shelf. Nikki still couldn't see his face.

"Anyway," she went on, after another deep breath, "I was wondering how you'd feel if I . . . well, if I went out with somebody else." There, she thought. I've said it. The worst is over.

Finally Tim stepped back from his locker. He was smiling casually as if they'd been discussing a homework assignment instead of their relationship.

"Well," he said, tucking a book under his arm, "it's not like you and I are seeing each other right now, is it? So if you want to see somebody else, I guess it doesn't really matter."

The worst wasn't over, Nikki decided. *This* was the worst. Tim's casual, ho-hum attitude was the last thing she had expected. Didn't he care at all?

Without warning, Nikki's eyes filled with tears. Blinking furiously, she turned her head away. She started to say something, but there was a huge lump in her throat. She was trying to swallow it when she felt Tim's hand on her arm.

"Listen, Nikki," he said, very softly. "I didn't mean to sound so cool about it. It's just that, like we said, neither one of us knows what we want to happen between us, right?"

Still swallowing hard, Nikki nodded.

"I think we need some kind of cooling-off time while we figure everything out," Tim went on, his voice still gentle. "But we can't just turn into hermits. So if you want to go out with somebody, fine. In fact, maybe it's a good idea for both of us to see other people. Not that I have anybody in mind," he added quickly. "But maybe it'll help us figure out how we really feel about each other, okay?"

Nikki nodded again. "Okay."

Tim leaned down and peered into her eyes. "You're sure?"

"Sure I'm sure," Nikki said, managing a smile. "I was the one who brought this up, remember?"

"Right." Tim gave her arm a little squeeze. "Okay, I've got to go. See you, Nikki."

After he left Nikki leaned against his locker for a minute. Kids rushed past her, hurrying to classes, but she hardly noticed.

She hadn't expected it to hurt so much, and that surprised her. It had been her idea, and here she was, blinking back tears. That could mean only one thing: she still cared about Tim Cooper. And if she did, then she had no business getting involved with anyone else. Not even if that person was Niles Butler.

School was almost over for the day, and Karen wasn't sure what to do. She'd never been the most decisive person in the world, but this was ridiculous.

DeeDee wouldn't waffle back and forth like this, she told herself as she headed down the hall toward her French class. As for Brittany, ha! Brittany would have had the story written by now.

If it were anyone but Ben who'd asked her to wait, Karen knew she wouldn't have a problem. Why did it have to be Ben?

"Why?" she said out loud as she walked into class.

"Why what?" somebody right behind her asked.

"Oh, Lacey, hi." Karen laughed. "I guess I was talking to myself."

"Don't worry," Lacey said. "I do it all the time, so I understand."

Karen laughed again. She liked Lacey. Some people—well, Brittany Tate, to be specific—thought she was an airhead and called her Spacy Lacey. But Karen knew better. Lacey Dupree might look as if her head were in the clouds, but her feet were definitely on the ground.

One more opinion, Karen thought, and then she would have to make up her mind.

"Lacey," she said as they got to their desks, "before Mr. LeBlanc comes, I need to ask you something." Quickly, keeping her voice low, she explained her situation again.

"Karen, it's awfully hard to give advice when I don't know the whole story," Lacey said. "But from what I can tell, you don't know the whole story, either. You say it's something bad. Well, if it is, then before you write a single word, I think you ought to be completely sure it's true. And if it *is* true"—Lacey smiled and shook her head—"then it's up to you whether to write it or not. Nobody can decide that for you.''

Marc LeBlanc hurried into the room just then, speaking rapidly in French.

Karen sat back, glad she'd asked Lacey what she thought. Lacey had made more sense than anybody. Of course, she did have to find out if the story was true. That's what the newspaper business was about—facts.

Karen didn't have that much experience following leads, but she thought she could do it. She knew just where she'd start, too—with Neil Lorrens.

 **6**

River Heights is out to win,
Come on, Bears,
Sink it in!

Led by Erik Nielson, the River Heights High cheerleaders whirled and clapped and cheered their basketball team on. The crowd chanted along, then leapt to its feet as Jerry Kuperman got one more basket before the halftime buzzer went off.

"Way to go!" Jeremy Pratt shouted, raising a clenched fist in the air as the teams ran off to the locker rooms. "I really think Coach Shay's going to take them all the way to the state championship this year."

Kim tucked her arm through his and laughed. "First they have to win this game," she reminded him.

"Oh, they'll win it." Jeremy sat back down and stretched his long legs out on the empty bleacher seat in front of him. "Eighteen points ahead at halftime? The other team doesn't stand a chance."

Turning to Samantha and Brittany, who were sitting with them, Jeremy said, "A win tonight will make my party. We'll turn it into a celebration."

"Mmm," Brittany murmured, nodding vaguely.

"I'm hardly a sports fanatic, but this is exciting," Samantha commented to Brittany after Jeremy and Kim left to get some water.

"Mmm," Brittany said again.

So much for conversation, Samantha thought. Brittany had hardly said a word all night, about anything. Her mind was obviously somewhere else. Which was a good thing after all, Samantha decided. Brittany hadn't noticed when Kyle had waved to Samantha from the bleachers below. Neither had Kim, thank goodness. She'd been too busy discussing Jeremy's party.

As the pom-pom squad ran onto the floor for their halftime routine, Samantha settled back and thought about how Kyle might look after their trip to the mall. She still wasn't sure what style would be best for him—preppie? Fifties retro? Scanning the bleachers, Samantha suddenly noticed Nikki Masters. Then she saw the guy sitting with her.

Now, there's somebody with style, she thought admiringly. It didn't hurt that he was extremely good-looking, of course, with that dark reddish brown hair and great build. But she was more interested in his clothes at the moment. Jeans and a soft, rust-colored shirt. The shirt looked very expensive, but the jeans kept him from seeming stiff or dressed up. Casually elegant, that's what it was. Maybe it would work for Kyle.

Samantha poked Brittany in the arm. "Did you see that guy with Nikki Masters?"

"I saw him," Brittany said flatly.

"And?"

"And what?"

"And what do you think of him?" Samantha pressed.

"Oh. He's very good-looking," Brittany murmured.

"Is that all you have to say?" Samantha asked, exasperated. "Are you sick or something? He's gorgeous."

"I've just got something else on my mind," Brittany told her.

"That's obvious," Samantha remarked

with a sniff. She paused. "What is it?"

"I can't tell you. Not yet," Brittany said. "But I promise, it's a lot more exciting than Nikki's latest acquisition." She smiled mysteriously and stood up. "I think I'll stretch my legs a little before the second half starts, okay?"

"Sure." Samantha was curious, but not enough to keep asking questions. Whatever Brittany was up to, she'd find out soon enough. In the meantime, she had the transformation of Kyle Kirkwood to think about.

Making her way down the crowded bleachers, Brittany didn't even glance at Nikki Masters and her friends. She'd noticed the new guy, of course—right away —but finding out about him would have to wait. Right now, she had a story to get.

Brittany had kept an eye on Karen Jacobs during the first half of the game. Karen had been sitting with her brainy friend, Teresa, but when halftime came Teresa had gotten up and gone out into the hall. Then Ben Newhouse came over and sat down next to Karen.

Now was Brittany's chance. People were moving around the bleachers, and there were a couple of empty spaces right behind

Karen and Ben. They might be talking about the cheating story, and if they were, Brittany was determined to hear every word.

As she slipped into the empty spot behind them, the pom-pom squad was just finishing its routine, and the band was taking a break. The gym was as quiet as it was going to get. Perfect timing, Brittany thought, and she leaned forward as far as she dared.

"Good game, isn't it?" Brittany heard Ben ask.

"It's great," Karen agreed. With Ben sitting beside her, it could have been the most boring game in history.

"Listen," Ben said, "I've been thinking. Remember that story we talked about?"

Karen nodded, her heart sinking. Was this why he'd come over to sit with her?

"I had an idea," Ben went on. "There's a lot of pressure in school these days — almost everybody's worried about grades and getting into a good college — and some kids panic. They'd do just about anything to make the grade."

"I know that," Karen said. "But —"

"Wait." Ben touched her on the arm.

"What if you wrote something about that instead? You could mention cheating in other schools. It'd be sort of like a warning." He leaned closer until their heads were almost touching. "An article like that might make whoever's doing it here at River Heights think twice. It might even make them so nervous they'd stop."

Karen wasn't sure what to say. Ben's idea wasn't bad, but if there really was a schoolwide cheating ring, it would probably take more than a subtle warning to stop it.

Before she could reply, Ben stood up. "Well, anyway, think about it," he said. "I'll try to come up with some other ways to deal with it, okay?"

Karen nodded. "Okay."

"Listen, Jeremy Pratt's throwing a big party tonight after the game," Ben said. "If you don't have any other plans, would you like to go?" He smiled at her, his brown eyes warm and friendly.

Karen's heart skipped a beat. He was actually asking her for a date! Was he finally over Emily, his girl who'd moved to New York to become a model? He had to be. If he wasn't, he wouldn't be asking Karen out, would he?

"I'd love to go, Ben," Karen said, her heart skipping another beat.

"Great," he said. "I've got my car, so I'll meet you right after the game."

He wants to be with me, Karen thought, watching Ben go back to his seat. She couldn't wait to tell Teresa. She didn't notice when Brittany Tate stood up behind her and started climbing up the bleachers.

Brittany was extremely frustrated. She'd been hoping for a lot of juicy details. But Karen had hardly said a word, and Brittany had no idea what was going on in her mind. At least Ben had invited Karen to Jeremy's party. Maybe Brittany would be able to get more information then.

Brittany liked Ben Newhouse, but she couldn't help wishing he'd mind his own business. Karen was obviously crazy about him, and she just might decide to give up on the story.

Brittany couldn't let that happen. She needed that story, and Karen was going to give it to her, whether she knew it or not.

Leon's, a popular pizza place, was always extremely busy after games. Before Nikki and her friends even walked in the door, they could hear the crowd inside laughing and shouting.

"Kuperman, Kuperman, he's our man!" everybody hollered. "If he can't do it, nobody can!"

Jerry Kuperman, freshly showered and grinning triumphantly, waved his hands in the air while all the kids stamped their feet and cheered again.

"It gets kind of wild after a game," Nikki said to Niles, standing inside the door. "Especially a game River Heights has won."

"I don't mind the noise," Niles told her, as he looked around the crowded room. "In fact, for pizza, I'm prepared to endure much worse."

"Don't tell me they don't have pizza in England," Robin teased.

"Oh, they have it," Niles said. "But it's not the same at all. I visited the States once before and couldn't get enough. I even took some back with me." He laughed. "Unfortunately, it doesn't travel well."

"Then you've come to the right place," Calvin Roth said. "Leon's makes the best pizza in town, right, Rick?" he asked Lacey's boyfriend.

Rick Stratton nodded. "It's great," he said with about as much enthusiasm as a rock.

Lacey frowned and took his hand. "Are you okay?" she murmured, so the others couldn't hear.

"I'm fine." Rick ran his other hand

through his hair, acting distracted. "I'm just—"

"Just what?" Lacey asked, hoping he'd finally open up and talk to her.

"Nothing." Rick shrugged. "Nothing."

"I see an empty booth," Robin called out. "Quick, let's grab it!" Reaching for Calvin's hand, she pulled him in a snaking pattern around the tables to the back of the restaurant. Lacey and Rick followed. Nikki and Niles stayed behind to order.

"How do you like it?" Nikki asked as they got in line at the counter.

"Absolutely chock-full of everything," Niles said. "Except anchovies."

"Thank goodness," Nikki said. "I hate anchovies."

"Really?" he replied. "That makes two things we have in common—liking photography and hating anchovies."

"How about tennis?" Nikki asked.

"I come from Wimbledon," Niles reminded her. "Need I say more?"

"I guess not," Nikki said with a laugh. "We'll have to play sometime while you're here. The country club has two indoor courts."

"I'd enjoy that," Niles told her. "Now," he added, "let's see if we have anything else in common. For instance, you've offered to show me around River Heights tomorrow, but what about tomorrow night? Do you have any plans?"

Nikki shook her head.

"Amazing," Niles said. "I haven't, either. And since your grandfather has kindly given my family a temporary membership in the country club, I'd like very much to take you to dinner. Will you come?"

For a second, Nikki thought of Tim. But only for a second. Looking at Niles, she smiled into his thick-lashed eyes and said, "I'd love to have dinner with you."

Jeremy's party was already in full swing when Karen and Ben arrived. Karen knew the Pratts were rich, but she hadn't realized exactly what that meant until she stepped into what Jeremy called the media room. A movie-size television screen covered most of one wall. There was a pool table near another, and an enormous stone fireplace on a third. Soft, oversize modular seating had been pushed back to make room for dancing on the Italian-tile floor, and rock music blasted from speakers in the ceiling.

"Enjoy!" Jeremy told them, gesturing toward a table laden with sandwiches, cold shrimp, three kinds of salads, and a huge tub filled with ice and cans of soda. "But you'll have to help yourselves," he said with a laugh. "My parents are out of town, and it's the maid's night off."

"His parents are out of town?" Karen asked, as she and Ben walked over to the food table. "And they let him have a party?"

"They must not know," Ben said. "Jeremy's going to be in big trouble when they find out. Come on, let's eat something in case it gets wild and we have to leave."

The party was loud, but it wasn't wild at all. Everyone seemed to be having a great time. Except Samantha Daley, Karen noticed. She was sitting in one of the low chairs, swinging her foot back and forth while Kim was talking to her.

"Come on, Samantha," Kim was saying. "Get on your feet and dance. There's Rob Steinberg." She pointed to a blond-haired guy filling his plate with shrimp. "He's not drop-dead gorgeous or anything, but he's not bad. And he's alone."

"Maybe later," Samantha said.

"Suit yourself." Kim shrugged and moved off to say hi to Tanya Peterson and Josh Rainer, two juniors who'd just arrived.

Samantha stared into the fire and thought about Kyle. It was too bad he wasn't there, but maybe after their shopping trip the next day, he'd be ready to make his debut.

"Hey, everybody!" Erik Nielson shouted when the music stopped. "Let's hear it for the team!"

"Let's hear it for Coach Shay!" someone else hollered.

The coach wasn't there, but some of the team members were, and everyone cheered loudly. Then Jeremy put another CD on, and the dancing started again.

Brittany Tate, looking great in a silky blue blouse and pants, spotted Karen and Ben talking together by the food table.

"Listen, Erik," she said to the handsome blond cheerleader she was dancing with, "I'm completely out of breath. Let me get something to drink and I'll come right back, okay?"

"Sure." Not missing a beat, Erik turned to another girl and kept on dancing.

Tossing back her dark hair, Brittany threaded her way through the crowd until she was standing near Ben and Karen.

"Hi," she said breezily. "Having fun?"

"So far," Ben said. "I hope Jeremy plans to shut this down before his parents get back."

"Oh, he will," Brittany told him. "He

knows he could get in trouble. But he decided to take a chance."

Brittany turned to Karen. "How about you, Karen? Are you having a good time?"

"Sure." Karen smiled and glanced down at her gray corduroy skirt. She wished she'd known she was going to Jeremy's party. She could have worn something a little less mousy.

"You know," Brittany said to her, "I've been thinking about that new advisor for the *Record*. I hope he's as good as DeeDee said. Maybe he'll assign us some really meaty stories."

"I thought you loved the stuff you write," Ben remarked.

"Oh, I do," Brittany said. "But I'd love to do some real tough reporting, too. Investigative stuff, you know? Wouldn't you like that, Karen?"

Karen stared at her. Did Brittany know something? "I guess it would be fun," she said slowly.

"Not just fun," Brittany said. "It would be a big help, too."

"What do you mean?" Karen asked.

"Well, think about it." Brittany's dark eyes sparkled. "Whoever wrote a big, important, investigative story would make a great impression on the new advisor. In fact, it might make him choose that person to be next year's editor in chief.''

Smiling innocently, Brittany picked out a can of soda and started walking away. But she stopped halfway across the room and looked back.

Ben was filling his plate and had his back to her, but Karen Jacobs was staring into the fireplace. Even from halfway across the room, Brittany could see the determination in her hazel eyes.

Good, Brittany thought with satisfaction. I reminded her that I'm the competition. She's got to do that story now, or she won't stand a chance against me as editor in chief.

Karen was going to start investigating the story, Brittany just knew it. And once she started, she'd have to keep a written record of what she'd learned. Names, dates —everything would be written down.

When Karen had the information, Brittany would figure out a way to get a peek at it. Then she'd run with it—all the way to the top position at the *Record.*

"Do you want a soda or something?" Erik Nielson asked.

Samantha shook her head. "No thanks."

"So, what did you think about the

game?'' he asked, sitting beside her on the modular sofa.

"Fantastic," Samantha said with a shrug. "River Heights has a great team this year."

Erik had been trying to get her attention all night, and now he had her cornered. Erik wasn't terrible—just kind of boring and dumb. He was great to be seen with because he was so gorgeous, but definitely no one to talk to. Also, Samantha didn't have time to lead him on. She was caught up in her plan for Kyle.

An electronic tone interrupted their conversation.

Saved by the bell! Samantha thought with a smile.

"What's that?" Erik said.

"Sounds like a phone," Samantha said, barely keeping the sarcasm out of her voice. She glanced around her. "The question is—*where* is it?"

The furniture had been shoved to the edges of the room to create a dance floor. There was no telling where the phone had ended up.

Erik stepped over a leather hassock and peered at the floor-to-ceiling bookshelves. He finally found the cordless phone stuck between a book and a bronze statuette.

"Here it is!" he said. "Should I answer it?"

Couldn't this guy decide anything for himself? Samantha looked around the crowded room for Jeremy. The house had filled up with party guests. It seemed that everyone—everyone who counted, anyway—had made it to Jeremy's party.

A flash of blue caught her eye. It was Brittany Tate, twirling around on the dance floor. She was dancing with Jeremy.

"There he is!" Samantha said, pointing. "But I don't think he wants to be interrupted. Why don't you just answer it?" she suggested.

With a shrug, Erik picked up the cordless phone. "Hello?" he shouted into the mouthpiece. "Hello?" He covered his other ear to block out the noise.

Samantha could see he was having trouble hearing the caller. It was no wonder. The party had gotten so loud, she could barely hear the music.

Jeremy had promised a terrific time, and no one could be disappointed with the outcome. Things had gotten a little out of hand at one point, though.

When two of the players from the basketball team had started a battle cry, one of them had grabbed onto the drapes, as if he were going to climb them. The heavy satin panel had ripped right across the top and fallen to the ground.

Samantha and Kim had been shocked. But Jeremy didn't seem to care.

"Don't worry about it. The maid will take care of it," he'd said.

And the music and laughter had continued.

Now Samantha wondered what Jeremy's parents would say if they could see the colossal mess that had been made of their expensive home. Sticky soda had been spilled on the expensive Italian-tiled floor, and the furniture was littered with crumbs and half-eaten sandwiches.

Mr. and Mrs. Pratt wouldn't be happy about the condition of their house. But then if Jeremy cleaned up and kept things under wraps, they might never know.

Erik was still trying to talk on the phone. "No," he shouted into the mouthpiece. "Mr. Pratt isn't here. Sorry." He hung up the phone and shrugged. "It was somebody calling for Jeremy's father."

Samantha nodded, trying to think of a way to make a graceful getaway from Erik Nielson.

Erik had just returned to his seat when the phone rang again. This time he made an agile leap over the footstool and snatched up the phone on the second ring.

"I told you," he said, "Mr. Pratt isn't here. He's out of town." After a slight pause, he added, "You'll have to speak up. There's a wild party going on here, and I can barely hear you."

"Oh, now I get it. *You're* Mr. Pratt," Erik said into the mouthpiece.

What? Samantha couldn't believe her ears. That was Jeremy's father on the phone! She jumped to her feet and started waving frantically at Erik.

But Erik just ignored her. And with each word, he dug Jeremy's grave a little deeper.

"Sorry, Mr. Pratt, but I can barely hear you. Oh, it's not just the music. This place must be filled with a hundred screaming people," Erik explained.

"Erik!" Samantha tried to stop him.

"Where's Jeremy?" Erik went on. "Why, he's right in the middle of the dance floor. He's a real party animal."

It was no use. Erik was such a lughead that he didn't realize he was getting Jeremy in trouble. He was on a roll, and there was no stopping him now.

"Well, I hope you're enjoying your vacation," Erik was telling Mr. Pratt.

Now was Samantha's chance to beat a hasty retreat—before Erik got off the phone and tried to monopolize her again.

Samantha turned around and started to squeeze her way through the crowd. It was time to hit the refreshment table and grab a sandwich. She might as well enjoy the rest of the party—it was bound to be the last one Jeremy Pratt ever threw.

7

It was Saturday, and the mall was packed, but Samantha had no trouble spotting Kyle. He was sitting on the low stone wall around the indoor fountain, fading into the background, as usual. Gray pants this time, and a light blue sweater that was too tight. Hadn't he ever heard of oversize clothes? Didn't he notice what everyone else was wearing? He must walk around with blinders on.

Samantha adjusted her dark glasses, reached up to make sure the bright paisley scarf she'd used to hide her hair was still wrapped like a turban, and headed for the fountain. Kyle might be smart, but fashionwise, he was a total illiterate. Today was the day to give him a true education.

"Kyle," she said brightly when she reached him, "I love the way you're always on time. You must get awfully tired of waiting for me."

Kyle stood up and peered at her. "Samantha?"

"Of course, it's me," Samantha said. "Didn't we have a date?" She put her hand on his arm and leaned close. "You weren't expecting anyone else, I hope," she purred.

"No, no," he said quickly, blushing. "I just didn't recognize you at first." He glanced at her scarf. "That looks nice," he commented. "I like your hair better, though."

Samantha did, too, but the scarf was necessary for the moment. There were too many people there that she knew. "Well, I like to try different styles," she said. "Clothes can be a lot of fun, you know. Dressing can be an art form."

Kyle shrugged. "I've never been too interested in clothes."

"Well," she said breezily, "the mall is a great place to start. In fact, why don't we do that?"

"What, buy clothes? It sounds kind of boring. I'd rather check out the record stores," Kyle said. "And I really want to look at a new computer program I'm thinking of getting."

"We'll do that, too," Samantha assured him smoothly. "But trying on different styles, seeing yourself in a completely new look—it's like a game, and it's a lot of fun." Samantha raised her dark glasses and smiled at him. "Shopping for clothes doesn't have to be boring, Kyle. Especially when you're with somebody you like."

"Okay, Samantha." Grinning, Kyle held up his hands in a helpless gesture. "I'm all yours."

"And that," Nikki said, gesturing from the window of her Camaro, "is the River Heights Mall."

Niles leaned toward her, looking out the driver's window at the parking lot. His face was so close, Nikki could almost count the lashes on his eyes.

"It looks busy," he said.

"It is," she told him. "It's Saturday. Cruising day."

"Cruising?"

"Well, kids don't go there just to buy things," Nikki explained. "We go to walk around, run into people, see what everybody else is up to, maybe make a date for tonight. Do you want to check it out?"

"Why not?" he said. "If I'm going to live here for several months, I should definitely learn the art of cruising a mall."

By the time they'd found a parking space and gone into the mall, Nikki and Niles were starving. When she'd picked him up earlier, Nikki had driven him out by Moon Lake, where they'd each shot an entire roll of film.

From the lake they'd driven back into town, with Nikki pointing out several places that kids liked to hang out. Then they'd gone to the park, both of them using up more film.

Now it was two o'clock in the afternoon, and Nikki had been about to take Niles home. But they hadn't eaten any lunch, and a hot dog sounded great to both of them.

They bought two each at Franks & Fries and stood together at the counter, eating and watching the crowd pass by.

"I see what you mean about cruising," Niles said, putting mustard on his second hot dog. "This is a place to see and be seen, isn't it?"

"Exactly," Nikki agreed. Though she wasn't exactly flaunting him, she couldn't help noticing how many kids were "see-ing" Niles at the moment, and she didn't blame them. He was easily the best-looking guy in the entire mall.

This fact had not escaped Samantha, who was passing by the hot dog stand with Kyle. Nervous, she quickened her pace and turned her head the opposite way until she and Kyle were around the corner. She didn't think Nikki would gossip about her and Kyle, really. It was Kim and Brittany she had to watch out for. Still, she couldn't be too careful.

Around the corner, Kyle spotted his favorite computer store. Samantha decided to wait outside while he browsed. Computer programming was not her thing. Besides, she wanted to get a better look at the guy with Nikki.

Adjusting her scarf, Samantha leaned around the corner. Fifteen feet away, heading in her direction, was Kim Bishop. When Kim saw Samantha, her blue eyes narrowed.

Samantha ducked back fast and made a beeline for the computer store. Once inside, she picked up a pamphlet and pretended to read it.

There was Kim now, walking fast, glancing all around as if she were looking for someone.

Samantha raised the pamphlet to cover her face. After a minute she peered over the top. Kim had stopped. Then she shrugged and walked on.

A very close call, Samantha thought, reaching up to her scarf again. It was coming undone; she'd have to go into a store and try something on so she could use the dressing-room mirror to fix it. She'd better do it fast, too, before she ran into Kim again. She might not be so lucky a second time.

"Mind if I stop in here?" Niles asked Nikki. He was standing in the doorway of Photofest, the mall's largest camera store. "I could use some more film."

"Good idea," Nikki agreed. "We went through a couple of rolls this morning."

"Can I help you?" the clerk asked.

Niles told her what type of film he needed. Then he asked the clerk to show him a special filter in the display case.

"How can I refuse, when you ask in such a charming way?" the clerk said with a smile. She seemed delighted with Niles's accent.

While Nikki waited, she realized how lucky she was that things had worked out this way with Niles. It would have been a completely different story if she hadn't hit it off with him.

Niles paid for the film, and they continued their tour of the mall. They were passing by a bookstore when a familiar face caught Nikki's eye.

It was Tim. He was sitting on a bench, talking with Doug Lynch. His gray eyes seemed to light up when he saw Nikki. He started to wave, then froze a moment later when he noticed that she wasn't alone.

Nikki's heart flip-flopped in her chest. The minute she saw Tim, all the old feelings came rushing back. She remembered the times when they had been inseparable. They had planned their schedules so that they could spend every spare moment together.

But those days were over, weren't they? Tim had told her that she should see other guys. So why did she feel so guilty browsing in the mall with Niles?

"Do you see someone you know?" Niles asked curiously.

"An old friend," Nikki answered. She hoped her face didn't reveal her embarrassment, but she felt an uncomfortable warmth creeping up her neck. "Let's go over and I'll introduce you," Nikki said.

Nikki tried to act nonchalant, as though it were no big deal introducing her former boyfriend to another guy. But deep inside, she felt awful. Would Tim think that she was a fast worker? That she was so boy crazy she had gone out and found another guy as soon as they had agreed to see other people?

"Hey, Nikki! Over here." Doug Lynch motioned them over.

"Hi, guys," Nikki said. Her heart pounded as she introduced Niles to Tim and Doug. "Niles is visiting from England. He'll be living in River Heights for a couple of months."

"England?" Doug said, shaking hands with Niles. "I guess we must sound pretty strange to you, then."

"A little," Niles agreed. "But then again, I'm getting used to your American slang. Any country with *hot dogs* and *hangouts* can't be all bad."

"Welcome to River Heights," Tim said stiffly. "How long have you been in town?"

"Just a week or so. Nikki's been showing me around, and she's a great tour guide." Niles flashed Nikki an appreciative smile.

"I bet she is," Tim said. His words were innocent, but his eyes were lit with anger. He looked at Nikki as if to say, "You don't waste any time, do you?"

Nikki felt as if she'd been stabbed right through the heart. Did love always have to hurt so much? Nikki wondered. She had always tried to be honest in her relationships. But sometimes it was hard to know how to act—especially when your feelings for a certain guy were confused.

She wanted to explain to Tim that this whole thing had started out innocently. In fact, she and Niles were just friends. It wasn't as if she had had another guy waiting in the wings while she and Tim were still seeing each other.

Taking a deep breath, Nikki was ready to explain how Niles's father worked for Masters Electronics. But before Nikki had a chance to offer any explanation, Doug and Tim were saying goodbye.

"Let's hit it," Doug said. "I want to get that new Dead Beats CD before it sells out at the record store." He shoved his hands in the pockets of his jacket and stood up. "See you later, Nikki. Nice to meet you, Niles."

Tim seemed eager to get away as he followed his friend. "See you around," he said, his handsome face pale, as if someone had knocked the wind out of him.

For a minute Nikki wondered if she'd made a mistake. Maybe she shouldn't be spending so much time with Niles. Tim had acted so betrayed and hurt to see her with another guy.

But then she glanced over at Niles and

noticed his carefree, easy smile. No, she wasn't doing anything wrong. After all, she and Tim had decided to take time off from seeing each other. She was right to spend time with other people—even if it made Tim a little jealous.

"They seem like nice guys," Niles commented. "You know, Nikki," he said as they walked past another shop, "I think I'm going to like it here in River Heights."

When Niles spoke with his British accent, things didn't sound the least bit corny. In fact, all his words were beginning to sound downright romantic.

Her scarf securely back in place, Samantha waited outside a dressing room in Just Gents. Kyle was inside, trying on pants and a sweater, both of which Samantha had picked out. Kyle still didn't seem interested in changing the way he looked, but at least he was going along with her and trying things on. The trick now was to get him to buy something.

Samantha was flipping through a rack of shirts when she felt a tap on her shoulder. She cringed. If it was Kim, there would be no way to fool her at such close range. She reached up, pulled her dark glasses back down over her eyes, took a deep breath, and turned around.

"Well?" Kyle asked. "What do you think?"

Samantha flipped the glasses back up and stared. The pants—soft, pleated, washed denim—fit perfectly. And the sweater was beautiful. A loose-fitting blue-gray wool with off-white yarn running through it in a swirling pattern.

Kyle looked down at himself, then back at Samantha. "No good, huh?"

"No *good?*" Samantha couldn't believe it. Except for the shoes and the hair, Kyle Kirkwood was not bad-looking. "Kyle, didn't you see yourself in the mirror? You look fantastic!"

"Yeah, well . . ." Kyle blushed and tugged at the neck of the sweater. "I thought I looked okay, but the way you stared at me, I wasn't sure."

"I was just speechless for a second," Samantha said. "Really, Kyle, that outfit is great."

"Yeah?" Kyle's face grew red as he gave her a big smile. "You know what? I think I'll buy this stuff. I won't have enough for that computer program, but who cares, right?"

"Right," Samantha agreed quickly. That was easy. Now for the next step. She moved back a little and scrutinized him, frowning slightly.

"What?" Kyle asked. "Did you change your mind about the clothes?"

"No, of course not. The clothes are fine." Samantha hesitated. "I was just looking at your hair." Smiling, she stepped close to Kyle. "You have such nice hair. It's really thick and shiny."

"You think so?" Kyle ran his hand through it. "It needs cutting, I know."

"Well . . ." Samantha pretended to think about it. "You might be right. If you're interested, I happen to know the Clip Shop is having a special this weekend."

Kyle laughed. "Why not?" he asked. "Like I said, I'm in your hands. Lead the way."

The Clip Shop was right next to Blooms, the flower store Brittany's mother owned. Brittany worked there sometimes to help out. Unfortunately, Samantha didn't remember that until they were almost right in front of it. Out of the corner of her eye, she saw Brittany inside, talking to a customer. Samantha took Kyle's arm and tried to hustle him past the shop.

"Wait a second," Kyle said, stopping smack in front of Blooms.

"What for?" Samantha glanced in and saw Brittany staring out the window. She turned her back on the store. "Kyle," she said, "when the Clip Shop has a special, it gets really crowded. Let's not waste any time."

She gave Kyle's arm a tug, but he didn't budge. "Let's go into that flower shop," he said.

"What? No!" Samantha almost shrieked. She couldn't go in there with Kyle. Not yet. He'd bought the great clothes, but he wasn't wearing them, so he still looked the same. "I mean," she said, lowering her voice, "the last time I was in there I knocked over a huge potted plant. It turned out to be really rare and expensive, and I ruined it. I paid for it, but I'm still too embarrassed to go back yet."

"Oh. Okay, you wait here, then," Kyle said. "I'll be right back."

Still looking over her shoulder, Samantha watched him go into Blooms. What was he doing? He knew who Brittany was, of course, and he knew she was Samantha's friend. Suppose he got into a conversation with her and just happened to mention that he was with Samantha?

Nervously chewing a fingernail, Samantha saw Kyle talking to Brittany. Brittany didn't seem to be listening. Instead, she kept glancing out the window in Samantha's direction. Fortunately, there was a giant fern on the counter, so her view couldn't be that clear.

Just to be safe, Samantha moved on down the corridor, her back to the flower shop. Once she was safely out of sight, she slumped against the window of the Clip Shop. Her scarf was giving her a pounding headache, and she was sick of her stupid dark glasses that made everything green. Was all this really worth it?

Then a minute later Kyle was walking toward her, smiling. When he reached Samantha, he handed her a beautiful red rose, its long stem wrapped in thin green paper.

"For you," he said. "I wanted to give you something beautiful."

Pushing up her glasses, Samantha took the rose. A deep, velvety red, it was just beginning to unfold. She smiled at Kyle, and her headache magically disappeared. Yes, she decided, Kyle was definitely worth all the extra work.

8

That night Niles glanced around the dining room of the River Heights Country Club. "This is quite a change from hot dogs at the mall," he said, smiling across the candlelit table at Nikki. "And from Leon's. I enjoyed both of them, although they're very different from what I'm used to."

"You mean you and your friends don't hang out?" Nikki asked.

"Not exactly," he said. "I go to a boarding school, you know, and it's near a small village—no pizza place or mall. Just a pub, where we can't go. During holidays, I go to lots of great places in London, but they're not the same as your hangouts."

"Well, you'll get used to it," Nikki told

him, buttering a roll. "Are you nervous, Niles? About starting school here on Monday, I mean."

"Terrified," he said, and smiled at himself. "That's an exaggeration, of course, but I *am* nervous. It's normal, I suppose. I'm afraid everyone already has their own friends and won't have room for another one. I'm afraid people will snicker at my accent."

"Are you kidding?" Nikki shook her head. "People will love your accent, take my word for it. It's very"— she started to say "sexy" but changed her mind— "attractive," she finished.

"That's good to hear," he said. "That you find it attractive, I mean." He smiled at her again, his eyes sparkling in the candlelight. "Speaking of attractive, I like your dress very much, Nikki. A black dress and blond hair are a great combination."

Nikki felt her heart thumping with happiness, but all she said was, "Thank you." She picked up her fork and dug into her salad. Why was she acting as if she were in love or something? Niles said she looked nice; he didn't say he was crazy about her.

She didn't want Niles to be crazy about her, anyway, did she? She wanted them to be friends. Now that she thought about it, they already were. The whole day had been so much fun. They'd talked about photography and tennis and school as if they'd known each other for years. And when they weren't talking, Nikki never felt desperate, as if she had to think of something to say.

So why did she feel so fantastic, just because a friend had paid her a compliment? Did she want Niles to be more than a friend?

"Anyway," she went on, "you met Lacey and Rick and Robin and Calvin last night. They didn't make you feel left out, did they?"

"Not at all," he agreed. "They were very warm and welcoming."

"See?" Nikki said. "You already have four friends."

"Five," Niles corrected. He reached across the table and touched her hand. "Don't forget yourself, Nikki. I certainly won't."

"Five," Nikki murmured, staring at their hands and feeling a blush creep up her face. Was he flirting with her or just being nice? And why did she wish he'd leave his hand on hers?

This is ridiculous, she told herself, sliding her hand away and picking her fork up again. It was time to tell him about Tim and get everything out in the open.

"This is kind of funny," she said, trying to sound as casual as possible, "but I met my boyfriend almost exactly the same way I met you. He was new in school at the beginning of the year, and I showed him around, too."

Niles didn't seem terribly disappointed when she'd said the word *boyfriend*. "Actually, he's not my boyfriend anymore, I guess," Nikki went on. "We kind of split up. I don't know if it's for good or not."

"I see," Niles said. "It must be a difficult time for you. Not knowing exactly where you stand, not sure about going back, but not ready to go forward to someone else."

"That's exactly the way I feel," Nikki said, grateful that he hadn't made her spell it out.

"I think I understand," Niles told her. "After all, here I am in a new school—a school with girls—but I don't feel free to fall in love or even begin dating."

"Oh?" What did he mean by not being free? Nikki's heart started to sink.

Niles shook his head. "I have a girlfriend in England," he said. "Gillian's her name. I already miss her very much."

"Oh." Nikki knew she should have felt

relieved. Everything was out in the open now. Even though she was attracted to Niles, and she was pretty sure he was attracted to her, neither one of them would do anything about it. She wasn't ready, and he had Gillian. Things were very clear. So why did she feel so disappointed?

On Monday morning Karen sat at her desk in humanities, fidgeting with her pen and trying not to watch the clock. She'd taken awful notes and knew she'd have to borrow somebody else's later, but she was too nervous to pay attention.

That day, she had decided, she would start her investigation. She knew she couldn't just walk up to Jerry Kuperman or Neil Lorrens and ask them if they had cheated, though. She was going to have to act her way through this and hope they believed her.

Finally Mr. Viera stopped talking and walked back to his desk. Picking up a pile of papers, he said, "Okay, I graded your tests over the weekend."

"Uh-oh, here it comes!" Tina Jenson, a jittery, dark-haired girl, giggled nervously and started chewing a fingernail.

"Please, please," lanky Drake Abrams muttered melodramatically. "An eighty-five, that's all I need. An eighty-five."

Mr. Viera chuckled. "Actually, some of you did better than I expected. Of course, some of you did worse." He chuckled again. "But overall, the class did pretty well."

There were some sighs and some whoops of happiness as Mr. Viera handed the tests back. Karen was dying to see if Neil was one of the whoopers, but it was time to go into her act.

When Mr. Viera dropped the test on her desk, she took a quick look—she'd gotten a ninety—slapped her hand over the score, and then slumped down, hanging her head and hoping she looked devastated.

The bell rang a minute later, and then Ben was standing beside her desk. "Bad score?" he asked sympathetically.

Karen didn't say yes—she couldn't bring herself to lie to Ben. Instead, she kept her hand over the score and said, "It could have been better."

"Hey, don't let it get you down," Ben told her. "Listen, I have to run, but I'll talk to you later, okay? Try not to worry."

When he was gone, Karen stood up and slumped toward the door. Right behind her was Neil Lorrens. He was whistling cheerfully.

Just outside the door, Karen stopped,

stuffed the test into her bag, and sighed loudly. Still whistling, Neil walked right into her.

"Oh, sorry, Karen." He peered at her curiously. "Karen? You okay?"

"Oh . . ." She shrugged. "It's just that . . . I didn't do so well on the test. And I really needed a decent grade."

"Really? I always thought you were good in humanities."

"I was, at first," Karen said. Actually, she had a ninety-two average so far, but she wasn't big on class discussion, so Neil had no idea what kind of student she was. "But all of a sudden, my grades started going down," she went on, putting a little quiver into her voice. "And not just humanities, either. I don't know what's happening! I work pretty hard, but I just can't seem to pull a decent grade. If my grade-point average gets too low, I'll be in big trouble."

"I know the feeling," Neil told her easily.

"You do?" she asked. "Why, did you do badly on the test, too?"

"Not really," Neil said, his blue eyes crinkling in a smile. "This time, I managed an eighty-eight."

Ha, Karen thought. Even cheating, he didn't beat her.

"But I wasn't doing very well for a while, and I really needed this grade to stay on the basketball team," Neil told her.

"Well, I'm glad you got it, then," Karen said, forcing a small smile. She wished she could make her eyes fill with tears, but it was impossible. "I'm not sure what I'm going to do, but . . . well, anyway, thanks for being sympathetic, Neil. I guess I'd better let you get going."

Karen started to walk away, shoulders hunched.

"Karen, wait up!" Neil called.

Thank goodness, she thought.

Neil took her arm and pulled her over to a bank of lockers. "Listen, Karen. The truth is, I got a little help on this test," he said in a low voice.

"You mean a tutor?" Karen asked innocently.

"Not quite," Neil said. He cleared his throat and shifted his eyes left and right. "I'm not sure how they do it. I think maybe they've got help in the office."

"How who does what? Neil, what are you talking about?"

Neil glanced around the hall again, looking nervous. "Listen," he said, lowering his voice even more. "You know Jerry Kuperman, right?"

Karen nodded. "Sure. But what——"

"He's the one you should talk to," Neil told her. "I'll speak to him first, and tell him you need to see him. He'll help you out, I'm sure."

"You mean he's a tutor?" Karen asked, pretending to be as confused as possible.

"No, but he can help get your grades up." By now, Neil was almost whispering. "He—and some others, I don't know who they are—can get hold of tests. Ahead of time."

Karen took a deep breath. "I'm really desperate or I wouldn't even consider it," she said, not wanting to sound too eager.

"Yeah, that's the way I felt," Neil said. "It's not right, I know, but I've only done it this once. Now that I'm back on my feet, maybe I won't have to do it again."

"So what makes you think Jerry and the others have help in the office?" Karen asked carefully.

"I'm not sure, but when I first talked to Jerry about this, Linda Rhodes was with him," Neil said. "You know her?"

Karen nodded. Linda was in her English class.

"Well, Linda works in the office," Neil said. "She has access to the files, so I just started wondering. But like I said, I'm not sure."

Karen decided not to ask any more questions. She didn't want Neil to get suspicious. Besides, they both had to get to their next classes. She took another deep breath. "Neil, you're a lifesaver," she told him. "Will you talk to Jerry for me — right away?"

"Sure," Neil said, smiling. "He's in my next class. Maybe you can see him at lunch."

"Thanks, Neil."

"Glad I could help," he told her. "Catch you later, Karen."

Once Neil was out of sight, Karen pulled a small notebook out of her purse and wrote down his name, Linda and Jerry's names, and the word *office* with a question mark next to it. Then she slipped the notebook out of sight.

She felt very strange all of a sudden. She hardly knew Neil at all, but he seemed like a nice guy, and she had stood right there and lied to him. He had no idea that she could get him into very big trouble.

But she couldn't start thinking about that yet. There was a lot more to this story, and she had to get the information. Then she'd decide what to do with it.

9

Samantha was ready to scream. Here it was lunchtime already. The cafeteria was packed, and Kyle still wasn't there. He'd gotten a great haircut on Saturday, and he'd promised to wear his new clothes. It was hard to believe, but she actually couldn't wait to get a look at him. She was dying to watch everyone's head turn when Kyle walked into the cafeteria. Where was he, anyway? She didn't want to have to wait until French class to see him.

"Samantha, will you please stop tapping your foot?" Kim said. "It's driving me crazy."

"Me, too," Brittany said, peeling her

orange. "What's the matter with you, anyway?"

"Not a thing," Samantha told them. "It's just a bad habit, I guess."

Kim looked more closely at Samantha. "That's a new sweater, isn't it?"

"Mmm," Samantha said, her eyes on the cafeteria doors.

"Top Drawer, right? When did you get it? Saturday?" Kim asked.

"Saturday?" Samantha gulped and reached for her milk carton. "No, not Saturday."

"Oh." Kim shrugged. "I thought I saw you at the mall."

"That's funny, I thought I saw you, too. I was working at Blooms," Brittany said, wiping orange juice from her fingers with a napkin. "But it must have been somebody else. This girl had a really tacky scarf wrapped around her head."

"So did the one I saw!" Kim said. "Isn't that weird?"

"Weird," Samantha agreed, laughing a bit too loudly. "I guess I must have a double."

"Hey, who's that?" Kim said suddenly. "He looks kind of familiar."

Samantha and Brittany looked in the direction Kim was pointing, and there was Kyle Kirkwood. His sandy hair looked great, short on the sides, longer and straight across at the back. The new clothes were perfect, casual but classy.

Samantha shook back her curly hair and trilled her fingers at him. When Kyle spotted her, he broke into a smile and headed straight for her table.

As Kyle walked toward her, several girls stopped eating and stared at him admiringly. Samantha noticed, of course, and she felt fantastic. Kyle Kirkwood was actually causing heads to turn!

"Hi, Samantha," he said when he reached their table. "I'm sorry I missed you this morning. I got a late start."

"That's okay." Kim and Brittany were gaping, Samantha noticed. Trying not to laugh, she said, "You remember Kyle Kirkwood, don't you? He tutored me in French."

Speechless, Brittany and Kim just nodded and smiled.

"Well," Samantha said, standing up. "I think Kyle and I will take a little walk before classes start again. Do you mind?"

Like puppets, her friends shook their heads and watched Kyle and Samantha walk away.

"Is something wrong with those two?" Kyle asked as they left the cafeteria. "They sure were quiet."

"Overwhelmed is the word," Samantha told him, smiling to herself. "They've never seen you looking so good. Neither have I," she added, slipping her arm through his as she walked proudly down the hall.

By the time Kyle and Samantha were out of sight, Kim had found her voice. "That's not really the same Kyle Kirkwood, is it?" she asked Brittany. "The Kyle Kirkwood I remember is a complete washout. Imagine Samantha being interested in somebody like that."

"Except he's not like *that* anymore," Brittany pointed out.

"Oh. Right." Still frowning, Kim said. "You don't suppose Samantha had anything to do with his transformation, do you?"

"I think she had everything to do with it," Brittany said. "Somehow she got him to buy some decent clothes and get a haircut that doesn't look like his mother put a bowl over his head and chopped away. And now she has a cool-looking guy who's crazy about her. Very clever."

"Hmm." Kim thought for a moment. "But Kyle was such a nerd," she said. "Do you really think some new clothes and a decent haircut could change that?"

Brittany didn't answer.

"Do you?" Kim asked, turning to her.

Brittany was on her feet. "Gotta go," she said.

"But we've got twenty minutes left," Kim protested.

"Sorry. Dump my tray for me, will you?" Brittany called back over her shoulder as she hurried away.

Left alone, Kim shook her head and peeled off a slice of Brittany's half-eaten orange. Her two best friends were acting very strange lately.

Hurrying across the crowded cafeteria, Brittany kept her eyes fixed on Karen Jacobs. Something was happening right now, she could feel it. Karen had been sitting by herself, when Jerry Kuperman stopped by her table to say something to her. After he left, Brittany could still see him. He went into the hall and stood there, glancing over at Karen every couple of seconds. Then Karen had finally gotten up, darted quick glances around her as if she were ready to commit a crime, and joined him in the hall.

The two of them were talking now, and Brittany was practically positive it had to do with the cheating story. Jerry was a jock, definitely not Karen's type. Normally they wouldn't have two words to say to each other, but there they were, heads together, chatting up a storm.

Just as Brittany reached the door, Jerry took Karen's arm and pulled her down the hall away from the kids coming out of the lunchroom. Obviously they needed to be alone. There was no way Brittany could get close enough to hear what they were saying without being seen.

Determined not to let them out of her sight, Brittany parked herself just across from the cafeteria doors. Pulling out a notebook, she leaned against the wall and pretended to concentrate on her English notes. Every few seconds she sneaked a peek over the top of the notebook at Karen and Jerry. It was extremely frustrating, but it was the best she could do.

Down the hall from Brittany, Jerry put his hand against a locker and leaned close to Karen. "I have to admit, you're the last person I expected to need this kind of help," he said, a sparkle of amusement in his dark eyes. "I had you pegged as a brain."

"Well, it's not that I'm flunking out, exactly," Karen told him. "But I just . . ." She sighed and shook her head.

"Hey, you don't have to explain it to

me," Jerry said. "You'd be surprised how many kids need — well, a little boost."

"A lot, huh?"

Jerry nodded. "You know Penny Waltham, right? And Rick Sutton?" he asked. "They're seniors."

Thank goodness for Jerry's big mouth! Karen tried to look surprised. "I didn't think they'd ever need to chea — I mean, need help like this."

"It just goes to show you, nobody's perfect." Jerry chuckled.

Even though she was nervous, Karen managed to chuckle, too. She wanted to keep him talking. "When Neil told me, at first I thought it was just for guys on the team."

"Well, it started out like that," Jerry said. "Coach Shay wants the best, but the best don't always keep their grades up."

"Mr. Shay doesn't— Does he know about this?"

"Hey, he's not in on it, if that's what you mean," Jerry said. Leaning closer, he whispered, "But he's no dummy."

Karen nodded knowingly.

"Now, about you," Jerry said, checking his watch. "What do you need?"

"Chemistry," Karen said. "Mrs. Melado's giving a test tomorrow."

A group of kids walked by, talking loudly, and Jerry waited until they had passed. "Meet me in the gym at three-thirty this afternoon. I'll have the 'notes' with me," he told her with a wink.

Karen decided not to wink back. "Thanks," she said. "You're a lifesaver, Jerry."

"Okay, gotta go," he said, checking his watch again. "Oh, and one more thing."

"Yes?"

"I don't suppose you could 'lend' me twenty dollars?" he asked, winking again.

Karen pretended to be confused. Then she smiled. "Sure, Jerry. I'd be happy to." She did a mental check of her billfold. Thank goodness, she had enough. "I'll give it to you in the gym later, okay?"

"Great! See you." Cocky and confident, Jerry walked off down the hall.

As soon as he'd turned the corner, Karen dug into her bag for her notebook. She checked first to make sure he was really gone, then quickly jotted down the names he'd mentioned: Penny W., Rick S., Coach. Beside the word *coach*, she put three big question marks.

Jerry had been so sure of himself—and of her. He must think everyone was willing to cheat, or at least not to care if it went on. And he'd been pretty willing to talk. Karen was glad. If he'd been really closemouthed, she wouldn't have as much of a story.

Now, though, the story was really taking shape. She had names of people she could question. And later in the day, she'd have real proof—a chemistry exam, bought and paid for.

Flipping her notebook shut, Karen put it back in her bag and headed for her next class. By the next day she'd have to talk to Ben. Once he knew how big this was, she was positive he'd change his mind about breaking the story.

Interrupting her thoughts just then, Brittany Tate came running up. "Karen! Hi!"

Karen blinked in surprise because Brittany wasn't usually so friendly. "Oh, Brittany. Hi."

"I'm almost done with my column for this week," Brittany said. "I thought I'd finish it this afternoon after school. Are you going to be in the *Record* office later?"

"For a while," Karen told her with a shrug. "DeeDee got some new photos in, and we need to decide where they'll go."

"Okay, I'll see you later, then," Brittany said cheerfully.

Karen gave Brittany a halfhearted smile and wave as she turned the corner and walked toward her class.

Walking in the opposite direction, Brittany had her teeth gritted in determination. At least she knew where Karen would be this afternoon. Now all she had to do was figure out how to get her hands on that notebook.

10

After school Nikki spotted Lacey waiting for her at her locker. Her friend was frowning and nervously coiling a curl of red hair around her finger.

"What's up?" Nikki asked, joining her. "You look either very mad or very upset. Which is it?"

"Both," Lacey answered glumly. "Nikki, I just can't figure out what's going on with Rick. I don't know if he's angry with me or interested in somebody else—or what."

"I'm sure he's not interested in anybody else," Nikki said. "He's crazy about you, Lacey. You know that."

"Well, if he is, he has a funny way of

showing it," Lacey complained. "He's always studying, or so he says, and he never talks to me anymore. I don't mind if he's quiet," she said, as Nikki twirled the combination on her locker, "but he just acts like I'm not there."

"Why don't you come right out and ask him what's wrong?" Nikki suggested.

"I start to," Lacey said, "but then I get scared. Suppose he really is mad at me?"

"He's not—I'm sure of it," Nikki said. "Something must be bothering him, though. Honestly, Lacey, I think you have to sit down and talk with him."

"I guess you're right," Lacey agreed. "As soon as I calm down, I'll do it. Oh, look," she added, as Nikki started to shut her locker door, "there's Niles."

Quickly, Nikki grabbed the door and checked her face in the little mirror she had taped inside. Her hair could use a brushing, but she looked okay. As she shut the locker, she saw that just about every girl in the hall was looking at Niles. No wonder, she thought. With those eyes and that reddish brown sweater that set them off, he was hard to miss.

"Hi," Lacey greeted him. "How was your first day?"

"Fascinating. I think I'm going to enjoy

school very much," Niles replied. "I must admit, though, that I'm glad the day is over. I'm feeling a bit overwhelmed."

Lacey laughed. "Join the crowd."

"I thought a slice of pizza and a soda might help," Niles went on. "Would you two care to join me?"

"Oh, I can't," Lacey said. "Thanks, but I've got to go to work."

"Another time, then." Niles turned to Nikki. "Nikki, can I persuade you to come?"

Nikki didn't need any persuading. "I'm starved," she said. "Let's go."

Fuming, Brittany pecked away at her typewriter in the *Record* office. She'd told Karen her column was almost done, but it wasn't anywhere near ready. She hadn't even gotten an idea for it! The only reason she was there was to get a look at Karen's notebook—but so far, the girl hadn't budged and her purse was right beside her.

Heads together, Karen and DeeDee were bent over a pile of photographs. They'd been doing that for twenty minutes, and Brittany was getting extremely tired of typing "the quick brown fox" over and over.

Clicking her tongue as if she just weren't

satisfied with what she'd written, Brittany ripped the paper out of the typewriter, tore it up, and threw it away. Now she needed more paper so she walked over to the big cabinet to get some. As she opened the door, a pile of old photos fell out.

Annoyed, Brittany reached down to pick them up. As she started to stuff them back inside the cabinet, one of the photos caught her eye. Blushing at the memories it brought back, Brittany stared at it.

The photo was of her car—her former car, that is. At the beginning of the year, Brittany's father had given in and bought her a car. She loved him for doing it, but unfortunately, it was one of the worst-looking clunkers ever made. A real tin-can junkmobile. She couldn't bring herself to be seen in it, so she'd abandoned it in the school parking lot before anyone had a chance to find out whose it was.

Someone *had* found out, though. And that person had used this very photograph to threaten Brittany with exposure unless she stopped trying to break up Tim Cooper and Nikki Masters.

Until now, Brittany had thought Robin Fisher had blackmailed her. Or maybe Nikki herself. But there was a note clipped to the back of the photo, a note that read:

"DeeDee, thought you might want this for your files. Lacey D."

So, Brittany thought, it was Lacey. She hadn't thought the Mouse had it in her. Very interesting. Folding the photo in half, she carried it back to her desk and stuck it between the pages of her French book. It definitely did not belong in the files.

Karen and DeeDee were still talking about the next issue. But just as Brittany decided she might as well give up for the day, Karen suddenly glanced at the big clock on the wall.

"DeeDee, I have to leave for a few minutes," she said. "Can we finish this later?"

"Sure." DeeDee was frowning at a photograph. She hardly seemed to notice when Karen left the room.

Brittany noticed, though. She also saw that Karen had left her bag hanging over the back of her chair.

With a smile, Brittany got more paper, then went back to her typewriter. She didn't have much time. If she could only get DeeDee out of the office, everything would be perfect.

Outside the gym, Karen nervously checked in the pocket of her white corduroy pants. She hadn't wanted to make a big production of fishing around in her wallet for money, so she'd put the twenty-dollar bill in her pocket earlier. There it was, folded up tightly so nobody would notice when she slipped it to Jerry.

Now for the real proof, she thought, taking a deep breath as she pushed the gym door open.

The piercing shriek of a whistle filled the gym as she stepped inside. The members of the basketball team stopped and listened as Coach Shay ran a hand through his dark hair and pointed out everything they'd been doing wrong.

"Okay," the coach said, clapping his hands. "Five minutes, then we'll get back to work. And I want everybody looking sharp."

While the coach took a couple of players aside to talk to them, the rest of the guys flopped down on the bleachers.

Spotting Karen, Jerry Kuperman gave her a quick wave, picked up his duffel bag, and jogged over to her.

"Hi," he said, still breathing hard. "Nice timing."

Karen's hands were almost shaking for fear of being caught. But Jerry isn't even nervous! she thought in amazement. "Did you get it?" she asked.

"No problem." He grinned. Unzipping the bag, he pulled out some papers and handed them to her.

Feeling like a criminal, Karen took them and gave him the wadded-up twenty-dollar bill. The papers were folded, and nobody could tell what they were, but she wished she'd brought her bag to stash them out of sight.

"What should I do with them, afterward?" she asked, tapping the papers. "Do you want them back?"

"Nope. Those are copies," he said. "We've got some help in the main office."

Linda Rhodes, Karen thought, remembering what Neil had told her. "Well," she said, stuffing the papers into her pocket, and pulling her burgundy sweater down as far as it would go, "that was pretty easy, Jerry. Thanks a lot."

"My pleasure," he said. "Hope everything works out."

"I'm sure it will."

"Okay, I've got to get back," he told her, glancing over his shoulder. "Coach really wants us to win our next game."

"I'm sure he does," Karen agreed. But she wondered if the coach knew how he would get his win. That was something she wanted to find out. Right now, though, she had a stolen test in her pocket, and all she wanted was to get away before she got caught.

Just as Karen was leaving the gym, Brittany leaned back in her chair and yawned. "I sure could use a diet soda," she said. "Maybe the caffeine would wake me up." DeeDee was a soda freak—maybe she'd offer to go get them some.

DeeDee studied her curiously for a second. "I'm still not sure what you're doing here, Brittany. You told me the column was almost finished."

So much for that hint, Brittany thought. "Well, it was. But it wasn't quite right," she said, typing away again.

A few minutes passed, and then DeeDee said, "Listen, I've got to go to the bathroom. You're not leaving yet, are you? Karen's bag is still here. You never know —somebody could rip it off."

"Go ahead," Brittany told her with a wave. "I'll keep a close eye on it."

The minute DeeDee left, Brittany leapt up and crossed the room in three steps. She listened for a few seconds and didn't hear anything. The hall was quiet.

Her heart pounding, she slipped her hand into the bag and felt around until her fingers closed over the little spiral notebook. For a second she wondered if she should really be doing this. Then she decided the story was too important. She'd worry about right and wrong later.

She was dying to read the notebook right that second, but she didn't dare. She'd make copies and read it later. Hurrying to the door, she looked up and down the hallway. Empty.

Rushing to the small copy machine, her hands shaking, Brittany flipped the notebook open and got to work. There were only three pages of notes, but the machine seemed to take forever.

When the last sheet finally came out, Brittany grabbed the copies, gave them a quick glance to make sure they were dark enough, and put them facedown next to her typewriter. Then, running on tiptoe, she took the notebook back to Karen's bag.

Were those footsteps? Yes, somebody was coming. Brittany knew she had to hurry, but her hands were shaking worse than ever. She was in such a rush, she knocked the bag off the chair.

Scooping up the bag, she stuffed the notebook inside. At that moment Karen Jacobs walked into the room.

"Oh, Karen, hi!" Lower your voice, Brittany told herself. You sound hysterical. "Sorry, I wasn't looking where I was going," she said more calmly, putting the bag back. "I bumped into the chair, and your bag fell off. Nothing fell out, though."

"Oh. Okay." Karen patted the pocket of her pants and then walked back over to the photographs she and DeeDee had been studying.

Karen had a funny expression on her face, Brittany thought, but she didn't seem suspicious.

A few seconds later DeeDee came back. Brittany sat down at her typewriter again, but she was too keyed up to hang around.

"Listen," she said, putting the copies of Karen's notes in her bag. "I must have writer's block or something. I think I'll forget about my column for now and start fresh tomorrow."

"Sure," DeeDee said, without looking up.

"See you," Karen murmured.

Brittany slipped on her jacket, gathered up her books, and walked out of the *Record* office. Halfway down the hall, she stopped and took the notes out of her bag. As she started to read, her mouth curved into a triumphant smile.

Bingo!

11 ～～

"I suppose it wasn't quite right for me to invite you," Niles said as he and Nikki left Leon's and walked to her Camaro. "You're the one who had to do the driving."

"That's okay," Nikki told him. "But, Niles, are you going to be able to drive here in River Heights at all?"

Niles held open the driver's door for her. "I certainly want to," he said. "But I just turned seventeen and haven't been driving that long back in England. And we drive on the left side of the road."

"Do you have a license?" Nikki asked. "I mean, one to drive in this country?"

"I can just use my British license, but I'm a bit nervous about the whole thing,"

Niles admitted. "So I haven't driven here yet."

Instead of getting into the car, Nikki held her keys out to him. "You'll never get the hang of it if you don't try," she said with a grin.

"Nikki, I'd feel terrible if something happened to your car," Niles said. "Or to you, of course," he added.

"Nothing's going to happen," Nikki said, assuring him. "Come on, Niles, take us for a drive."

"As long as you insist," Niles said, reaching for the keys. "I'd be delighted."

Getting out of the parking lot was no problem, but once they were on the street, things got a little tricky. Pulling up to a stop sign, Niles said, "Where shall we go?"

"Let's drive out to the lake and back," Nikki suggested. "That way you'll do some town driving and some country driving. Turn left."

Niles pulled the car into the intersection, made a smooth left turn, and stayed on the left.

"Right," Nikki reminded him.

"Sorry, I thought you said left."

"I did, I meant keep right. Quick!" Nikki said, trying not to shout. "There's a car coming!"

Niles jerked the car into the right lane just in time. The driver from the opposite direction honked loudly and shouted something they couldn't hear.

"You don't suppose he was welcoming me to River Heights, do you?" Niles asked wryly.

Nikki burst out laughing. From then on, she reminded him to stay on the right, and they made it to Moon Lake with no trouble at all.

Karen checked her watch again and started pacing the hallway outside the room where the junior class meeting was being held. Ben was in there, and she had to talk to him.

She'd done what Lacey Dupree had suggested: She'd made sure the cheating story was true. Now she had decided she had to do something about it.

If it wasn't for Ben, Karen would have been busy writing the story that very moment. She was sure that once she told Ben what she'd learned, he would agree that she should write the story. He'd understand now that the story was too big to sweep under the rug.

Besides, if *she* didn't write it, Brittany Tate just might. That business with her purse earlier seemed awfully suspicious.

Karen wouldn't put it past Brittany to snoop in her things. It had been incredibly stupid to leave her purse unguarded with all her notes in it, but she couldn't do anything about that now. If Brittany had seen her notes, it wouldn't take her long to put the whole story together.

Finally the door to the meeting opened, and kids started leaving. Karen stationed herself right outside and took Ben's arm the minute he came out.

"Karen, hi," he said, acting glad to see her.

"Ben, I have to talk to you," she told him quickly. "But not here," she added. "Could you drive me home? We can talk on the way."

Usually, Karen would have been too unsure of herself to suggest that Ben take her anywhere, but this was too important. She couldn't be shy now.

"Something's up, I can tell," Ben said. "Sure, I'll take you home. Come on." The two of them walked out to the parking lot. Ben didn't ask any questions until they were in his car.

"I know something's wrong," Ben said finally, backing out of the parking space. "It's the cheating thing, isn't it?"

Karen nodded. "It's true, Ben. The story, I mean. When you asked me to wait on it, I decided I'd better find out if it was really happening. Well, it is." Karen took some papers out of her purse and held them up. "This is a copy of the chemistry test I have to take tomorrow," she said. "Jerry Kuperman sold it to me today for twenty dollars."

Ben listened silently, frowning, as Karen told him everything she'd learned. "It's not just one or two kids doing this," she finished. "It's a lot of them. I still don't know how many, but Jerry talks like they're running a business. I don't know exactly how they get the tests, either," she went on. "I was afraid to ask too many questions. But I'm sure I can find out. And, Ben, I even think Coach Shay may be involved in some way. Jerry said he's not, but I think he's at least aware that it's going on, and that's bad enough."

Karen took a deep breath. "I don't see how I can look the other way about this any longer. What's happening is wrong."

By now they were at Karen's house. Ben pulled the car up to the curb and shut off the engine. Turning to face Karen, he said, "I know it's wrong, but I still don't think you should write the article."

Karen started to protest, but Ben held up his hand. "Wait," he said. "I know you think you'd be doing the right thing. But,

Karen, what happens after the story breaks? Have you thought of that?"

"The cheating stops," Karen said.

"It's not that simple." Ben shook his head, his brown eyes worried. "The whole school would be ripped apart. Kids' lives would be ruined. Seniors would probably lose their chances for college, at least for a while. And everybody might be suspended. The basketball team would have to start from scratch, and if Mr. Shay does know about the ring, he'd be out of a job."

Karen had to admit, she'd never really thought about those things. She remembered Neil Lorrens and couldn't help feeling sorry for him. He'd only cheated one time—should his life be ruined because of that?

"I know there are students who are doing something wrong," Ben said again. "But I don't think kicking them out of school or wrecking their chances for college is the right way to go. They need help, and there's got to be another way to give it to them." He drummed the steering wheel softly. "Maybe the school should require tutoring when somebody's grades start to drop." He sighed. "I don't know, Karen. It's just that I know some of those kids you named. I don't want to see anyone get hurt, that's all."

Karen couldn't think of anything to say. If people were in trouble, Ben always wanted to help them, not get them in deeper. She loved him for that, and she wanted him to love her, too.

Maybe she was being selfish, wanting to write the story to help her become the editor in chief.

If she wrote the story, would she lose Ben before they had a chance to be a real couple?

"I can't believe it's this late!" Nikki cried, glancing at her watch. "Have we really been at the lake for so long?"

"I guess we have," Niles said. "Funny, it doesn't feel like a long time."

It sure doesn't, Nikki thought. The old saying about time flying was really true. She'd been having so much fun with Niles, tramping in the cold around Moon Lake and talking, that she hadn't even noticed how late it was.

"We'd better head back," she said reluctantly. They were watching the last pink streaks in the sky after the sun slid behind Moon Lake. "I have a lot of homework. Do you?"

"I'm afraid so," Niles said. "My teachers didn't show me one ounce of pity, even though it was my first day. I hate to leave here," he added.

"So do I," Nikki said, taking his hand to pull him along.

Niles kept hold of her hand for a second before he let it go.

"We'll have to come here again." Nikki could still feel the warmth of his fingers and wished Niles would hold her hand again.

She couldn't believe how disappointed she felt when he didn't. What was happening? Weren't they just friends? Hadn't they agreed that neither of them wanted to get involved?

As she sneaked a look at Niles's handsome profile in half light, Nikki felt her heart do a weird little flip-flop. *He* might not want to get involved, but she realized at that moment that she wasn't sure about herself anymore.

She'd fallen for him the first time she saw him, of course. He was so good-looking, anybody would have. But now, after spending more time with him, she thought she might actually be falling in love.

"Karen, you hardly touched your dinner." Mrs. Jacobs was putting a plate in the microwave for Karen's father, who wouldn't be home until later. "I hope you're not coming down with the flu. It's everywhere now."

"It's not the flu," Karen said with a sigh, getting up to clear the table. "I'm just tired, I guess."

Mrs. Jacobs poured herself some coffee. "You do look tired," she said. "You look worried, too."

Karen said nothing.

"Want to talk about it?" her mother asked.

Karen suddenly realized that she did. Maybe her mother could solve the whole thing. She put the plates into the dishwasher, then sat back down at the kitchen table and told her mother everything.

Well, not exactly everything. She didn't say what her big story was about, because she was afraid her mother would insist that she go right to the principal. But she made it clear that something wrong was going on, that she knew about it, and that Ben didn't think she should write about it.

When she'd finished, her mother sighed. "No wonder you're worried," she said. "Ben's really put you on the spot, hasn't he?"

"He's got a point, though," Karen said.

"He really cares, Mom. He doesn't want people to get hurt."

Mrs. Jacobs sipped her coffee and shook her head. "I don't know what to tell you to do," she said. "But, honey, whatever you decide, do it because it's what *you* want, not because a boy is telling you what to want."

Her mother hadn't solved the problem, but Karen hadn't expected her to. Nobody could—except Karen herself. The trouble was, she didn't know how.

12 ⌇

The sky was heavy with lead-colored clouds Wednesday morning, and they were growing thicker by the minute. Freezing rain or snow was obviously on the way, and the wind whipping around the quad made everyone huddle deeper into their coats. As usual, though, nobody wanted to go in until the last minute.

"Isn't this an absolutely wonderful day?" Samantha asked.

"Are you crazy?" Kim frowned and stuck her hands in the pockets of her white jacket. "It's freezing out here. My nose is bright red, I can feel it."

"It sure is," Samantha said cheerfully. "You look a little bit like a rabbit, in fact."

"How come you're so happy?" Kim asked. "I thought you hated the cold."

"Not today," Samantha said with a big smile.

"Oh, I get it," Kim said. "You're too much in love with Kyle what's-his-name to notice when the weather's rotten."

"Kirkwood," Samantha told her. "Kyle Kirkwood. Don't pretend you forgot. I have the feeling nobody's going to forget his name from now on."

"Okay, okay," Kim said with a laugh. "I have to hand it to you—he looks pretty hot now." She glanced around the quad and nudged Samantha in the ribs. "There he is, by the way, talking to those girls. Better watch out, Samantha. You might have some competition."

But it was obvious, even to Kim, that Kyle had eyes only for the pretty girl with the cinnamon-colored hair who left Kim's side and hurried toward him. The minute he saw her, he broke into a smile and left the other girls behind.

"Oh, Kyle, I'm so glad to see you," Samantha said when they'd reached each other. "And that jacket—it looks perfect."

"You ought to know." He laughed, looking down at his denim bomber jacket. "You pointed it out on Saturday. I went back and bought it last night."

Samantha tucked her arm through Kyle's. "Have you seen how people are staring at you?" she asked. "The girls especially. Do you feel any different?"

"I suppose I do," he replied. "I'm not used to being noticed, but I think I can manage." He shrugged. "It could even be fun."

"But not too much fun," Samantha warned, half joking.

"Don't worry about that, Samantha." A little awkwardly, Kyle bent his head and grazed her cheek with his lips. "You're the only one I really want to notice me."

By the time Karen was daydreaming through her humanities class, the freezing rain had started and the classroom windows were streaming with water. Tired from too many sleepless nights, she stared at the raindrops and tried to get her mind working. She still hadn't decided what to do about the story. If only she could solve the whole thing by flipping a coin!

She was trying to stifle a yawn when Mr. Meacham, the principal, walked in the door. The students exchanged puzzled looks while he had a short, whispered conference with Mr. Viera. They both were very serious.

In a few more moments the principal turned to the class. "Neil Lorrens, Ben Newhouse, Amy Levin? Come with me, please," he said

Suddenly wide-awake, Karen watched as the four of them left the room. Ben glanced at her and looked away quickly. What was going on?

Just before class was over, there was a familiar crackling sound from the loudspeaker on the wall. Everyone looked up. Soon the vice-principal's voice came over the PA system: "Two new announcements," she said. "This afternoon's cheerleading practice has been cancelled. Friday night's basketball game between the Bears and the Hawks has been cancelled. Repeat: Cheerleading practice and the basketball game have been cancelled."

Almost immediately the bell rang, and there was a buzz of excited conversation as everyone left the class. Her heart pounding, Karen joined the crowds in the halls.

"Karen!" Teresa called, running up to her. "Do you have any idea what's going on? Two people were called out of my calculus class just now, and somebody else saw Mr. Shay sitting outside the principal's office. They said he looked *totally* grim."

Before Karen could answer, she caught sight of Brittany Tate hurrying down the hall. Her eyes were bright with excitement, and she had a knowing smile on her face.

It has to be the cheating story, Karen told herself. What else could it be? The coach, Neil, the basketball game—it all added up. Except for one thing—Ben. He'd been called to the principal's office, too. But Ben couldn't possibly be involved in this. Or could he?

Brittany felt particularly good. This was what being a real reporter was all about: getting a lead, following it through, checking the facts. Of course, Karen was the one who'd actually discovered the story, but that was beside the point. It was she, Brittany, who was going to write it.

Still smiling to herself, Brittany turned a corner and startled Lacey Dupree, who was getting something out of her locker. Good, Brittany thought, she's alone. She watched as Lacey picked up the notebook she'd dropped. Brittany had something extremely interesting to tell her. One of the names in Karen's notebook was *Rick S.* And who else could that possibly be but Rick Stratton, the Mouse's boyfriend?

Lacey glanced at Brittany, frowning, and started to walk on.

"Oh, Lacey, wait," Brittany called after her, hurrying to catch up. "Something's going on today," she said breathlessly. "I guess you've probably noticed."

Lacey shrugged. "Yes, but nobody seems to know much," she said.

"Well, *I* happen to know a lot," Brittany told her. "But I can't go into any details yet. You'll read all about it in the *Record*."

Lacey stopped in her tracks and sighed heavily. "Okay. What's your point, Brittany?"

"My point is, don't be too surprised when Rick Stratton's name shows up in my story."

Lacey looked at her blankly.

"I hope you plan to stand by your man, Lacey," Brittany said sweetly. "He's definitely going to need somebody on his side."

Leaving a befuddled Lacey standing there, Brittany continued on her way. She'd paid the Mouse back for using that photograph against her. Now that she'd settled that score, she felt better than ever.

Karen had one more class to get through before lunch, and when the bell finally

rang, she was the first one out of the room.
By now, the entire school was buzzing
with rumors, but Karen knew the best
place to get the real scoop—the *Record*
office.

The minute Karen walked inside, she
knew she'd been right, and her heart sank.
DeeDee and Brittany were both hunched
over their typewriters, their fingers flying.
They were obviously working to add an
extra story to the paper, and it could only
mean one thing—the cheating story was
out.

DeeDee spotted Karen and threw her a
withering look. "I can't believe you sat on
this for so long, Karen," she said angrily.
"Not only is it a major story, but it's not
the kind of thing you keep quiet about. It's
a schoolwide cheating ring, Karen!"

Karen swallowed hard. "I was just trying to decide on the best way to handle it,"
she said, her lips feeling stiff.

"That's a lame excuse," DeeDee
snapped. "The minute Brittany called
me about it, I knew we had to go to the
principal. And we didn't wait until this
morning, either. We called Mr. Meacham
last night."

Suddenly Brittany let out a groan. "I
just wish Mr. Meacham had given us the
rest of the names," she said. "It would

make the story so much more sensational!"

Karen closed her eyes for a second. Brittany was having a great time; she didn't even seem to care that people were in major trouble.

"Brittany and I were in Mr. Meacham's office bright and early this morning," DeeDee told Karen. "By then he'd already gotten the whole story out of Jerry Kuperman and Linda Rhodes."

Karen's head was pounding, and she felt dizzy. She couldn't bring herself to ask if DeeDee knew whether Ben had been involved.

"By the way," DeeDee said, "Mr. Meacham did tell us that Jerry mentioned your name, Karen."

Karen shook her head. "I didn't . . . I was just . . ."

"Well, that's one thing you don't have to worry about," DeeDee told her. "Brittany told the principal you did it for the paper, to get the story. Buying that test was the right thing to do, at least. I just wish you'd told me about it right away."

Karen closed her eyes again. Was she supposed to be grateful to Brittany Tate after the girl had stolen her story?

"This is hardly the time to take a nap, Karen," DeeDee said scathingly. "Do you have the test? Mr. Meacham said it's okay to run a copy of it."

Silently, Karen took it out of her bag and handed it over.

"Well?" DeeDee said as she took the pages. "You're not planning to stand there forever, are you? We've got a paper to get out!"

Karen took one more step into the room, then turned on her heel and walked out. She had to get away from DeeDee's anger and Brittany's gloating. She didn't want to help out. She wished she'd never even joined the *Record* staff. All she wanted to do was to go home and crawl into bed.

By the time school was out, the rumors were still flying. Some kids said the entire student body was planning to go on strike for better food in the cafeteria. Others were convinced there'd been a bomb threat and wondered why school hadn't been dismissed early. Only a handful of students had heard the real story, and Robin Fisher was one of them.

"A cheating ring, can you believe it!" Robin said indignantly as she and Lacey walked outside together. "The rest of us break our backs studying, trying to get decent grades, while a bunch of lazy creeps buy theirs and coast along."

Lacey's heart dropped. "You mean it's really true?"

Robin nodded, her big hoop earrings swinging wildly. "Ellen Ming told me. And she would know. She's a junior class officer. The class officers and student council heard the whole thing from Mr. Meacham." Robin stopped and looked at her curiously. "How come you weren't at that meeting? You're secretary of the junior class."

"I had to skip it and study in the library. I've got a big research paper due in English," Lacey said. There was still freezing rain outside, but Lacey didn't even feel it. "You're sure, Robin?" she asked. "You're absolutely sure?"

"Positive." Robin pulled up the hood of her bright orange poncho. "They're doing a special piece on it in the *Record*," she said. "It's going to name names. If I were one of those kids, I wouldn't show my face around school tomorrow."

"So that's what she meant," Lacey said slowly, feeling cold and numb.

"What who meant?" Robin peered at her friend through the rain. "Lacey, are you all right? You're awfully pale. Well, you're always pale, but now you look kind of greenish."

"What?" Lacey hitched her book bag up

on her shoulder. "No, I'm not sick. Listen, Robin, I've got to go. I'll talk to you later, okay?"

Leaving a mystified Robin standing in the quad, Lacey whirled around and ran toward the student parking lot. She'd asked Rick to meet her there after school, just so she could see him for a few minutes before she had to go to work.

Lately, she'd done all the talking. Now it was Rick's turn.

"How's it going?" DeeDee asked. She handed Brittany a can of soda and sat down in the chair beside her.

"It's fabulous—if I do say so myself," Brittany said. She stopped typing for a moment to open her soda and take a sip.

"I'd like to start printing soon," said DeeDee. "A story this hot needs to hit the presses right away. I want to have it in this Friday's paper."

"No problem." Brittany leaned back and stretched out her arms. "Brittany Tate has never missed a deadline," she reminded DeeDee. And she would be sure to point that out to Mr. Green, the new advisor.

"I love it when a story comes together," DeeDee said with a sigh. She pulled her chair up to her desk and started to proofread an article.

"Thanks to me, we have a story," Brittany reminded her. "If we had waited for Karen Jacobs, we'd still be in the dark."

"Yeah," DeeDee murmured absently. The editor-in-chief was so engrossed in the article, she was no longer listening to Brittany.

A satisfied smile curled Brittany's lips. She could allow herself a moment to gloat over her own success—and Karen's devastating failure.

Oh, she'd had to resort to a few dirty tricks to accomplish her feat, but it was worth it. Even if it meant swiping Karen's notes and eavesdropping a little. A good reporter had to get her story—at all costs!

Returning to her typewriter, Brittany read the last paragraph she had written. Her eyes danced over the names of Jerry Kuperman and Linda Rhodes. So what if they were suspended from school? They were just peons, anyway. At least they'd go out with a bang. This was likely to be the hottest story of the year.

Brittany started typing another name, but hesitated. Her fingers paused over the keyboard as she thought about including the Mouse's boyfriend in the article.

Rick S. had to be Rick Stratton—didn't it? How she'd love to shock everyone with an extra scoop!

But then again, if she was wrong, she could be the laughingstock of River Heights High. All the glory and success of the cheating-ring story would be forgotten in light of her mistake.

Brittany frowned, then erased the entire sentence. Better to be safe than sorry. She couldn't let anything get in the way of this hot story—and her appointment as next year's editor in chief of the *Record*.

Besides, if Lacey Dupree's boyfriend was involved in the cheating scandal, he'd be discovered. Sooner or later.

"Okay," Brittany announced. "I'm ready to print."

13

It can't be true, Lacey kept telling herself as she ran through the soggy grass toward the parking lot. Rick couldn't possibly be involved in this cheating mess.

But if he wasn't, why had Brittany Tate said he was? She probably knew the names of everyone involved.

Of course, Brittany would hardly win any prizes for honesty, Lacey reminded herself. She was sneaky and underhanded. Look at the way she'd caused trouble between Nikki and Tim. She could be lying about Rick just for the fun of it. Lacey wouldn't put anything past Brittany Tate.

Still, Lacey kept remembering how quiet and preoccupied Rick had been lately. They were just juniors, but he'd already started worrying a lot about getting into a good college. He'd need a scholarship, and he had to have good grades for that. Could he have been cheating and feeling horribly guilty about it? That would explain a lot of things.

It just can't be true, Lacey told herself again. But she had to know, and the only one to ask was Rick himself.

By the time Lacey reached the parking lot, the hem of her long wool challis skirt was splattered with mud and her long wavy hair was bunched in wet clumps around her neck. Finally she became aware of the rain and fished around in her backpack for her collapsible umbrella and opened it.

There was Rick, slumped against his car, his hands stuffed in the pockets of his jeans. He didn't seem to care about the rain, either.

"We're both soaking wet," Lacey said as she joined him and gave him a kiss on the cheek. "Why aren't you sitting in your car?"

Shrugging, Rick wiped his hand over his sandy brown hair. "Didn't think of it, I guess."

So much for small talk, Lacey thought. She decided to come straight to the point.

"I guess you've heard about the cheating ring," she said.

He nodded, keeping his eyes on the ground. "Yeah."

Lacey took a deep breath. "Rick, I have to ask you something. But before you answer, if the answer is yes, I want you to know I'll understand. I mean, it would be terrible, but I wouldn't hate you."

She definitely wasn't getting straight to the point, Lacey realized. Another deep breath. "Rick, am I going to read your name in the *Record* tomorrow?" she blurted out. "Were you one of the people who cheated?"

There. She'd asked. Now she'd know for sure.

Rick raised his eyes and stared at Lacey. He was silent, and she had no idea what he was thinking.

Suddenly, though, his eyes changed. They glared at her with fury. Rick pushed himself away from the car and stood up straight. "I don't believe it!" he said, his voice shaking with anger. "How can you even ask me a question like that?"

"Rick, I—" Lacey began.

"Forget it!" he shouted. "Just forget it!"

Spinning around, Rick yanked open the car door and got inside. The engine roared to life. Without even a glance at Lacey, Rick drove out of the parking lot.

Lacey stood looking after him, wet and cold and miserable. He thinks I don't trust him, she thought. She had practically accused him of cheating. Would he ever speak to her again?

The rain had slowed to a drizzle by the time dinner was over. Not that Karen had eaten any of hers, but she could hear her parents downstairs, loading the dishwasher.

Karen was upstairs in bed, curled under the covers. That's where she'd gone the minute she'd gotten home from school. That was where she was going to stay. She knew her parents were wondering what was wrong with her, but she wasn't ready to tell them yet. She wasn't ready to talk to anybody. She just wanted to be alone.

There goes my chance at being editor in chief next year, she thought for the hundredth time. The new advisor was sure to hear about this fiasco. Even if he didn't, DeeDee would never recommend Karen now.

And even if Brittany hadn't stolen the story, Karen was the one who had sat on it for so long. She should never have done that. Cheating was wrong. She should have broken the story right away, and she'd probably known that from the beginning. But she was so afraid of making Ben Newhouse mad that she'd let him talk her into waiting. Not having done what she knew was right was even worse than losing her big chance at being editor in chief.

Then there was the awful possibility that Ben was involved in the cheating ring himself. He'd seemed so sincere, but was he just trying to talk her out of it to save himself? *That* would be the worst part of all.

Karen turned over under the quilt as a soft tap sounded at the door. Oh, great, she thought. Mom and Dad want to talk.

Another soft knock, and Mrs. Jacobs pushed open the door. "Honey?" she said. "How are you feeling?"

"Horrible," Karen said bluntly. "I'd really like to be alone, Mom."

"I realize that," her mother said. "But you have a visitor."

"Who?" Karen asked, frowning.

"Ben Newhouse."

Karen sat up. What was Ben doing here? "I can't explain everything right now, Mom," she said, "but I don't think I can face him."

"Well, I told him you weren't feeling well, but he refuses to leave." Mrs. Jacobs laughed a little. "Do you really want your father and me to throw him out of the house?"

"I guess not." Karen sighed. She might as well get this over with. After everything else that had happened, what was one more rotten experience going to matter? "I'll be down in a minute."

When her mother left, Karen threw back the covers. She combed her tangled hair with her fingers and tightened the belt on her bathrobe. It was an ancient, faded yellow robe, but she wasn't going to change. She was through trying to impress Ben Newhouse in any way.

Karen found Ben downstairs in the living room. Her parents were nowhere in sight, thank goodness.

Ben was standing in the middle of the room, looking nervous. When he saw Karen, he took a step toward her, then stopped. "Thanks for coming down, Karen," he said. "Your mother told me you weren't feeling well, but I had to see you."

"Yeah, well . . ." Karen stuffed her hands in the pockets of her robe. "I'm okay. I mean, I'm not physically sick. Feelings can make you sick, too, you know."

"Karen, wait a minute," Ben said. "Be-

fore you tell me how much you hate me,
just hear me out, please?"

Karen leaned against the doorjamb and
nodded.

"I wasn't cheating," Ben said flatly.
"I've never done it, and I never will. I
know what you must have thought when I
got called down to Mr. Meacham's office
this morning," he went on, "but it's not
true. You'll read some of the names in the
paper tomorrow. Mine won't be there."

He was telling the truth, Karen was sure
of that. Nobody could look so sad and
earnest and still be lying. "Then why were
you called to the principal's office?" she
asked.

"He wanted to tell me about it, since I'm
class president," Ben said. "He had all the
class presidents in his office. I guess he
wanted to let us know what was happening
before everybody else found out."

"Well, I'm glad you're not in trouble,"
Karen said. "I really am."

"But I am in trouble," Ben told her.
"With you. Because I made you wait for
the story, even though you didn't want
to." He shook his head. "See, Karen, the
truth is, I knew about the cheating, even
before you told me. I even knew how they
did it—they stole a key from the custodi-

an's key ring and made a copy. When you told me what you'd found out, I thought about warning everybody. But that wouldn't have been right, either. I guess I was hoping the whole thing would stop by itself. I didn't want to see anybody hurt. I know a lot of the kids who were involved."

"It seems like everyone knows at least one person who was involved."

"Yeah, it was a pretty big deal. The coach might even lose his job because he suspected that a lot of guys on the team were cheating and he didn't say anything." Ben started pacing around the room. "Anyway, the other reason I'm here is to tell you that I know I was wrong. You should have gone ahead with the story. I didn't just decide that after today, either," he said. "After I talked to you yesterday, I went home and did some pretty heavy thinking. You were right, Karen, and I feel rotten about everything."

Karen gave him a small smile. She was still mad, but mostly at herself. "I shouldn't have let you talk me out of it," she told him. "I guess we're even."

"You don't hate me, do you, Karen?" Ben asked anxiously. "I mean, I really like you a lot." He stopped pacing and stood in front of her. "Will you forgive me?"

"Just don't try to talk me out of doing

another story," Karen said. "If DeeDee doesn't get me thrown off the paper, that is."

"She was mad?" Ben asked.

"Freaked," Karen said. "And I don't blame her. I was really stupid to listen to you."

"I'm sorry, Karen," Ben said. "I really mean it."

"I know you do," Karen told him. "I still feel rotten, but I don't hate you, so stop worrying."

"Good." Ben moved closer to her. "This may be a bad time to ask, but do you think you could stand to go out with me again sometime?"

Karen smiled again. "I guess I could stand it," she said. "Thanks, Ben, for coming to talk to me."

Ben held out his arms, and Karen walked into them happily, tacky bathrobe and all.

It was almost midnight, but Lacey was still awake, worrying about Rick. Stop it, she told herself. You can apologize to him first thing tomorrow. If you don't get to sleep, you won't ever get up in the morning, and then you won't even see Rick at all.

She was just dozing off when her bedside

phone rang. Fumbling in the dark, Lacey picked it up.

"Hello?" she said groggily.

"Lacey?" It was a woman's voice, weak and shaky. "This is Mrs. Stratton."

Rick's mother! Lacey sat up and turned on her lamp. "Mrs. Stratton? What is it? Is something wrong?"

"I—" Mrs. Stratton's voice broke. "It's Rick, Lacey. He didn't come home after school, but we didn't start to worry for a while."

Lacey's heart was pounding and her mouth went dry. "What happened?"

"We're not sure exactly," Rick's mother said. "The police think he must have decided to go climbing around that rocky area out by the lake. Of course, he's a very good climber, but the rocks were so slippery from all the freezing rain." She caught her breath in a sob. "Lacey, he fell."

"How bad?" Lacey whispered. "How bad is he hurt?"

"It doesn't look good," Mrs. Stratton said. "The doctors aren't even sure. . . . Lacey, could you come to the hospital? I know Rick would want you here."

Lacey was already struggling out of her nightgown. "I'm on my way, Mrs. Stratton!" she cried. "Tell Rick I'm coming!"

Ten minutes later Lacey was in the car on the way to River Heights Hospital. She hadn't even told her parents; she'd call them from the hospital. Her parents could wait. Everything could wait.

Rick needed her, and that was all that mattered.

———

Rick lies unconscious, and Lacey is devastated. When he wakes up, will he be able to forgive her? Brittany is turning over a new leaf—no more scheming. Will playing nice help her snare a date with Tim Cooper to the Winter Carnival Ball? Find out in River Heights #8, *The Trouble with Love*.